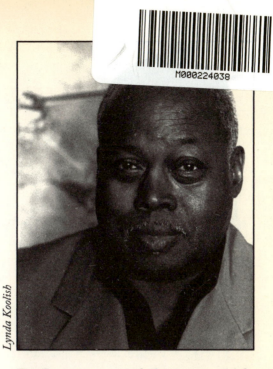

Lynda Koolish

ED BULLINS, one of the most prolific African American writers of his generation, has authored such works as *In the Wine Time, Goin' a Buffalo, Clara's Ole Man,* and *The Taking of Miss Janie,* which received the New York Drama Critics Circle Award for Best American Play of the 1974–75 season. He has also won multiple Obie Awards, Guggenheim fellowships, and playwriting grants from the National Endowment for the Arts, among other honors. Along with Amiri Baraka, Bullins is considered to be one of the key figures of the Black Arts movement. *The Hungered One* was originally published in 1971.

THE HUNGERED ONE

THE HUNGERED ONE

Short Stories by
Ed Bullins

with a preface by Amiri Baraka

AKASHIC BOOKS
NEW YORK

This is a work of fiction. All names, characters, places, and incidents are the product of the author's imagination. Any resemblance to real events or persons, living or dead, is entirely coincidental.

Published by Akashic Books
Originally published in 1971 by William Morrow and Company, Inc.
©1971, 2009 by Ed Bullins

ISBN-13: 978-1-933354-66-8
Library of Congress Control Number: 2008925943
All rights reserved

First printing

Akashic Books
PO Box 1456
New York, NY 10009
info@akashicbooks.com
www.akashicbooks.com

ALSO FROM AKASHICLASSICS: RENEGADE REPRINT SERIES

Home: Social Essays
by LeRoi Jones (Amiri Baraka)

Black Music
by LeRoi Jones (Amiri Baraka)
(forthcoming in fall 2009)

ACKNOWLEDGMENTS

This book would not be possible if it had not been for those *little magazines*, many now defunct, that allowed me to be published and to grow. Many thanks to *Black Dialogue, Citadel, Dust, Illuminations, Liberator, Manhattan Review, Nexus*, and *Wild Dog*. The contents of this book first appeared in their pages. Grateful acknowledgment is made to *Black World* for permission to reprint "Support Your Local Police," copyright 1967 by *Negro Digest*.

E.B.

To all my children

Table of Contents

PREFACE
by Amiri Baraka

Actually, Bullins's work is more subtle than he writes it. These are coarse stories, tales of rough-edged youth and frustrated adults. The main theme, or wire, running through these short muffled cries is frustration, seeing but not copping, copping but not digging, awash in the lost-and-found of this life shit and not knowing which one you is.

They seem like they have been hacked out of something—sprays of sand from dirt, showers of flakes from a block of ice, dust from the inevitable saw shaping us around our life, or maybe memory in its ghoulish detail, what we saw.

In that sense, they are as dry as Bullins most famously is, except he has brutalized that silence that surrounds him to say something about what he has dug in and of the world. This is a cold, hard, seedy world Bullins gives us. But we recognize it as part of our own. There are master works here, "Support Your Local Police," "The Hungered One," for instance, and others. But there is also an edgy silent harshness, a world held together by yearning and regret, where desire is met with smothered instinct, hope with mocking laughter.

Quietly touching, stealthily brain-rattling. Feeling

and thought, is what Bullins offers. However bitter, it's good for us.

The distance between what we want and what exists.

Amiri Baraka
Newark, NJ
October 2008

INTRODUCTION
Premonitions of a Monstrous Time

On a recent near-lovely autumn evening, I read my story "The Hungered One" at a literary gathering. During the Q&A segment of the program, naturally, I was asked where I came by this piece of writing. I answered that perhaps it was a premonition of some monstrous time that has now appeared. The moderator announced that its genre was allegory. I remained silent. And the audience seemed comfortable, having figured out this thing with the aid of the arbitrator. But was it all that? An allegory?

> . . . having hidden spiritual meaning that transcends the literal sense of a sacred text.
> —Webster's New Collegiate Dictionary,
> G. & C. Merriam Co., 1957

Prior explanations of the origin of my four-legged-creature story did not seem as important to skeptics—I would say that the beast came from a dream of mine, and premonitions are not necessarily dreams. So is "The Hungered One" about some kind of Western Freudian probing? Or is it all about allegory, that type of world literature which stands for something that is about other things that are not fully realized or expressed?

I do not entirely know what this story possesses in terms of symbols and significance, but it came into being fully formed, like its namesake, and was first published in 1971.

When I began writing seriously—which to me meant following in the footsteps of fiction writers like Richard Wright, Henry Miller, Eugene O'Neill, Walt Whitman, Ralph Ellison, Franz Kafka, Gwendolyn Brooks, Emily Dickinson, Jean Genet, James Baldwin, Chester Himes, Langston Hughes, Adrienne Kennedy, Jack Kerouac, Sonia Sanchez, John Guare, Marvin X, Edward Albee, Idries Shah, Ishmael Reed, and so forth—I fought with myself to make each new work, initially, as different from my previous writing as possible. I lost that early battle, though I know the attempt was sincere and worth the struggle.

I imagine now that I was trying to answer the voices of the Beat Generation: Allen Ginsberg, LeRoi Jones, Philip Whalen, Michael McClure, et al. And also through my early work I discovered "The Absurd One," which opens these writings, acknowledging the generation of Genet, the Theatre of the Absurd, Ralph Ellison, and the literary existential faddists of the late 1940s and '50s. The story "Moonwriter" comes straight out of the Haight-Ashbury coffeehouse culture of the late '60s, though L.A.'s Pogo's Swamp a decade before helped incubate these literary Happenings. My longtime friend Amiri Baraka showed me how to write "The Enemy" through his example. *Change! Change! Change!* we hear today, but how did hardened personalities like Malcolm X and Amiri Baraka become wise philosophers and prophets so quickly?

As a neophyte participant, a rank novice, I developed much like a boxer, an artist, or a sprinter who takes on an extreme challenge, or even a marathon player who might put his/her life on the line. A boxer can spar at the gym or in the back alley, and develop into a contender if he has the heart and will. The artist of music, studio painting, and sculpture (as well as installation art) can also develop in various ways. My own creative writing grew in a hopscotch kind of experimental way. By the time I got to "The Hungered One," I was taking full steps.

Being young and black in the '60s and '70s was a remarkable experience. As a writing student and soon-to-be editor of *Citadel*, the Los Angeles City College literary magazine, I met Malcolm X before he captured the headlines and minds of much of urban America. Along with other student leaders, I had been fortunate enough to have lunch with Martin Luther King, Jr. at LACC in the late '50s or early '60s. I remember the day that President John F. Kennedy was assassinated and my Contemporary Literature Club (of which I was president) huddled together and swore we would find a way to make this country a better place. (Can you believe how young we were?) I have met, befriended, shared living quarters and organized with numerous political, artistic, cultural, and progressive activists of the past fifty years through my writing and theater endeavors. And if I had to, I would do lots of it all over again (hopefully having learned more). And by the way, please understand that all of this relates to the universal paraphrase—for instance: *The past is the past, although what goes around comes around.*

I did not write a play until nearly a decade after I began working on stories in my early twenties. In this book, the vignettes "In the Wine Time" and "In New England Winter" became the prologues of the plays of the same names.

She passed the corner in small ballerina slippers, every evening during my last wine time, wearing a light summer dress with big pockets, swinging her head back and to the side all special-like, hearing a private melody singing in her head . . .

We picked Chuck up at noon and drove with brood hanging close to our bodies blended with the sweat. The '53 burped reliably in its infirmity; its windows gulped the grit which peppered my face, and Indian summer rode with us across the city, a spent brave, a savage to the last, causing me visions of winter in New England . . .

After I read dozens of plays, worked for a while as trashman and stagehand at little theaters, and then began trying to write my own plays, I found that incorporating some of my fictional work was of great help. *In the Wine Time* was my second full-length play, following *Goin' a Buffalo*. *In New England Winter* came in third place.

Soon I concentrated on dramatic writing, though I did have a novel published during the following years.

And this is part of my story as a writer. Surprising. It's the beginning of the tale with much more to follow. I would be happy if it never ended, but that's impossible, right?

Ed Bullins
Roxbury, MA
October 2008

PART ONE

THE ABSURD ONE

To Joe Wooly . . .
    from Mississippi . . .
    to Hate (Haight) Ashbury
    & death . . .
    filling his belly
    with life

The Absurd One

I have no understanding of how that absurd being whose lair is centered behind our eyes takes us over, stealing from his cave in our brains to take us over for a sliced second; but, in dream, when dog weary, in the d.t.'s or cold turkey we sometimes glimpse him, or better, his claw flexing, hinting of the Absurd One's eternal presence, his ironic whim for destruction or creation.

Some of us know him and are in an intimate compromise to his capture in that unsuspected interval, for we know he may call once a year in the dawn as we practice our art—that he viciously splashes a shadow of his perfection onto the canvas, upon the page or within the wood, stone or clay, and as soon, swipes back and withdraws and awaits his whim another year or more, and we are left madmen who scream futilely within, screams which reverberate in the Absurd One's hole, screams he gloats upon, screams he draws sustenance, for they are his solemn reverences, given by the devout and reverent believers. We scream inside for that impossible perfection he teased of.

Or the Absurd One may come in the bed and bite with our teeth through our love's nipple or into our manhood and he intimidates us both to lie of it as our love, or the Absurd One may prance with the punch of the needle, popped as he pursues the heart, until he is the heart, pumping, pounding to every portion, and you are he, awesome in absurdity. Or with the lung-scorched joint effect the Absurd One may lift out your mind from its case and insert an endless running bump-and-grind piano roll of creation until he becomes absurdly bored and sprinkles a pinch of depression into his bed, your head, before slamming back the brain, snapping the musical paper toilet roll of the universe, or the Absurd One may one day like the other days but for that day, slide down the out-of-uniform Royal Crowned and processed cowlick of the seventeen-year green sailor, into the forty-year breathing wide nostrils belonging to the scrawny whore who "moved like she had a propeller in her tail"; the same woman who shed a tear from dehydrated glands forgotten since twelve, the same woman absurdly taken in the crotch so as to have a twitch disbelieved since fifteen, the same who sliced forty-year veins after the boy was gone with his money still to be used for another skinny one, the same who blubbered the entire distance to the psycho ward that she had somehow felt absurdly impure when Joey, or was it Johnnie, or Moe, when it was unknowingly Sam, was with her with the exact mixed amounts of Mississippi sweat, lye, lard and sweet water that someone once had who had had her at ten in some absurd hayloft . . . of all places. But there was reality in his bumpkin bounding and pounding.

It then must have been the Absurd One who was there that one sliced second of night or day that you or me or we stood with glass in hand and with unshakable conviction in the arrogance of our convictions that the answers possessed were our own answers. It was he then who pulled the blinds behind our eyes, reversing them,

slipping the slats out and back again all at once, as your
eyes changed from brown to blue, from grey to white or
charred good black in the heat of possibility, when Absurd stood behind you that second that you knew you
were a girl or a boy though your Brooks Brothers and
Chanel spoke with proper authority otherwise, but the
Absurd One whispered in that absurd second that men
and women and girls and lads are all one and the same
as you and all look boss, to you, for you wanted a man
or a woman or a girl or a boy or yourself, which was the
best possibility, and you knew entirely, backed up by
Absurd, that you could then in that sliced second and
at once fuck the world, Sealy Posturepedic or not, for it
waited; it waited with mouth wide.

Moonwriter

On rainy Saturday . . . and there I was at one of them thar scary lit-ar-airy beer busts with real writers and he-man things . . . with sandals and beards and handlebar moostashes and tweeds and pipes . . . and agents and contracts and credits and the moon and mountains and in Mexico were in the room . . . with beer belches.

We put down all mutually known writers not there . . . unless, of course, they came later.

And there I was saying . . . "Yeah . . . and after bein' a bouncer in Naples and a bodyguard in Sicily I got to . . ."

"Yeah . . . you and the Mafia in Palermo . . ." someone said.

". . . and I got to Spain," I continued, "and ran into a hassle with the lightweight champ of that part of the world . . ."

But then I sighed fuck-it inside and didn't tell them that I've had a lot of odd jobs, my father ain't Italian, and all the champ and I did was get to like each other finally; he drank me under the table.

People dream of goin' to the moon . . . I'd just like to get back down into livin' . . .

Should I have dropped my pants and flashed bullet blister, round and pus pushing, sometimes sore on snowy days.

Should I have shined stiletto slash seam of stitches skimming jugular vein, or pursed pulled together punctures in back. Should I have flexed my scars and screamed: "But . . . mah pain is in mah brain . . . yawhl!"

Should I have said: "Check with J. Edgar . . . sweetie!"

But I shouldn't be blowin' 'bout the past; the past is with me each night hobbling on cloven hooves holding hands with dead dream masks that even drugs can't dim. They dance to goat songs sung until dawn in spirals about my head.

I lived by the gun . . . and know those who live will die . . .

I live a lie . . . and know those who live die . . .

I have notches on my soul . . . and know those who have . . . have . . . have need of death . . . for sleep has dreams and handholding songs.

I've met Death on ageless corners and died in streets without corners in Brooklyn, in Philly, in Hollywood, in Boston, in Nice, in Marseilles . . . on corners without streets.

I've woken up dead in drunk-tanks, on hospital slabs . . . never ever in bed.

I've notches on my soul . . .

the gun . . .

Notches . . .

the knife . . .

Notches . . .

You want to go to the moon, writer?

Go via Harlem, Dante.

Muses of mountains, poet, with sprinkles of waiting solitary secrets?

Sip a random sample of meatless everyday soup

in solitary stir with visions of tits, arse and better . . . scorching steel cells.

Romance in Mexico, *hombre* . . . with *advaanture* . . .

Tell your analyst elephant jokes, men, the punch line being: "Elephants don't fuck with analysts!"

The gun, the knife, the dream, the lie; notches behind my eyes.

My Id can lick yours anyday, moonwriter.

The Enemy

To Norm Moser

I am an enemy of the State. I do not mine bridges nor take over the national airways or private airlines at gunpoint. I do not preach revolution against the Republic in its overt dialectical forms. I do not even care what political elements make up the State at the moment, unless these factions jeopardize my personal desires, caprices or concerns. Nor do I care who holds the balance of power within the government. I simply do not care for the presence of the State; it is the supreme evil to my existence, for I am against all factions, groups, agencies and alliances which make up the State, and I know, not so secretly, that they are against me. For I am their constant threat, for I am in essence against everything the State purports to be. I stand against the institutions of the whiteman.

One can easily find me. I am on the streets of the cities. I walk and wait on streets with names like Broadway, Market, Central and Main. I stand huddled in stupor in the doorways of transient hotels, occasionally freeing myself from the shadows and pleading for pennies from pedestrians. I am found asleep in the early mornings, in the waiting rooms of bus stations, last night's newspapers my sheets, the black-booted policemen tapping upon the soles of my shoes with nightsticks, awakening me to arrest or sending me on my unknown way. I am seen peering for minutes at the billboards under the marquees of four-bit, all-night movie houses; my fingers in my last holeless pants pocket, rubbing my last two quarters together. Sometimes I look like a man, sometimes a boy, sometimes a woman, sometimes a girl. Sometimes I am none of these.

And at times I can be discovered inside, inside green and grey painted jails, pacing off the days and years in my dirt-colored cell. I sleep fitfully and wake screaming with nose bleeding, trembling, in drunk-tanks, until hauled desperately out and straitjacketed by annoyed guards in tan and grey uniforms. I lie awake inside of one-dollar-a-night flophouses, dreaming of old loves and clean smells. I sit up all night scratching bedbug bites and stalking juicy roaches in lonely rooms on skid row. I hear the bump bump de bump of the strip joints under my tenderloin window, the visions of the aging showgirls grinding and rolling up to my window like the din. From across the tracks the whistle of no longer scheduled trains reaches me, and the DIN din of the life buoy in the harbor and the bellow of ships shoving off to sea and the shrill work whistle at the plant that does not shriek for me, all this comes to where I sit, inside my deserted soul.

The Excursion

The wind was blowing that day. Not in high puffing breaths but steady, snatching at the woman's taut skirt as she sauntered along the street, stopping occasionally to straighten her stockings or to look back over her shoulder at a passing car, then begin walking again when the auto did not slow.

In the length of a block, several would draw up to the curb and the drivers would signal or honk their horns. Sometimes she would walk over and whisper with them and shake her head and step back upon the curb and begin her slow walk once more. Finally, she chose one and stepped inside as the car pulled away from the curb and spun around the first corner like a quick rodent. She sat huddled against the door, far from the driver who spoke to her with curt jerks of his head.

The car headed east driving through the sunny afternoon streets and turned onto an on-ramp of a freeway and moved into the flow of traffic. It speeded up and wheeled to the outside lane and speeded to the limit and took the bridge turnoff.

At the tollgate the cashier took the quarter and the car passed through. The driver headed over the pass with the mist spewing down from the crest like phantoms diving from the heights of the peak to the crystal bay at the base of the landscape.

Within an hour the car reached the park at the summit; a gate of huge redwoods welcomed them with twin signs carved from living wood. Deep into the six-foot signs were cut elongated NO's, standing vertically to the left, and smaller words lined up on the right side: smoking, fires, necking, spitting, feeding the animals, drinking, molesting visitors, cutting vegetation . . .

After parking, the couple followed a footpath leading into the interior of the park. Sounds of cheering and play came from behind a grove of trees and when the two circled the woods a ball park was found filled by people with bats and balls and gloves.

Hefty, crew-cut fathers, their bellies hanging across their belts, directed their sons and stepped forward when the young ones failed to perform superbly and took the bats away, smashing the small balls to sing across the field, with the young boys in sulking pursuit.

The man and woman sat in a cleared area and watched, but before an hour were made to move on by the stampeding lunges of the heavier ball players. The two walked down a wider path above a gully that had a large pool carved into it; signs were posted above the pool's fence. ALL THE FISH YOU CAN CATCH—NO LIMIT!—$1.00 AN HOUR WITH FREE EQUIPMENT. WE RE-STOCK OUR POOL HOURLY WITH LIVE GAME FISH! The woman looked down over the fenced pool, seeing the tee-shirted fishermen waiting patiently for a nibble. She and the man continued on up the hill to the pony ride.

The small animals were tethered to a wheel that turned as they dragged their hooves about the small rink. Small children were tied upon the saddles, after parents bought tickets, and the ponies were whipped to canter slightly faster at the beginning of each ride.

On the way back to the car the woman saw one of the fishermen pull a bright silvery thing from the pool; a crowd surrounded him and several hands patted him upon the back.

Dropping down through the redwood country the mist thinned and warmth broke the day's greyness.

It didn't take the auto long to reach the city. The Sunday traffic allowed the driver to reach the woman's street quickly. The machine swung to the curb and she stepped clear.

"Next Sunday?" the driver asked as she looked back.

She shook her head and started away.

"But we'll have longer," the driver called after her. "And the sun might shine all day."

She stopped and looked back. She shook her head again. The man stared and seemed about to speak.

"I just feel so filthy afterwards," she said. "Don't you understand?"

He pulled away from the curb; the big car was gone. She sauntered along the street, stopping occasionally to straighten her stockings or to look back over her shoulder at a passing car, then begin walking when the auto did not slow.

An Ancient One

Under a grey sky the ancient woman feels like an insect along the cement walk in front of the cream and green building. The building wears a green tiled roof and green trims the windows and the maple door, and the old woman searches at its base with her slender brown cane, feeling forward with head bent low from her humped spine, hovering over her feeler, a grey spider.

She passes the house's grey speckled steps, the black specks contrasting with her long dark grey coat almost sweeping the ground. A matching colored hat—a brimless grey straw hat—with a black felt ribbon pushes over her white head, and no green curtain or shade in the house flutters, shakes or raises as she passes.

It is an olive-green building she creeps up to, stopping briefly to peck her stick at a tumbling brown paper blowing by. Then she continues up the incline to the stoop of the olive-green building with its twelve marble stairs, and crawls secretly up each, clasping her cane under right armpit and strangling the rusted iron guide rail to claw her way up.

Her house is trimmed in white; white curtains wait at each window like poor relatives. She stoops at the top landing, peers into the mailbox, and feebly inserts her dark brass key and flutters through the nest's opening.

The Reason of Why

My coffee is cool. I sip at my cup and carry my plate into the kitchen, placing it in the newly scrubbed sink. With lukewarm coffee filling my cup, I walk from the kitchen, cross the living room, back into my tiny sleeping area, and pull the covers across my mattress. I grab up my loose socks, towel and other garments lying about the edges of the mattress, and stuff them into a partially filled pillow case in a corner at the head of my pillow. A frown is fought back as I return to the front room.

I sit at the old, borrowed Underwood. The paper waits blank in the carriage. To the right of the machine lies a clipboard, empty, ready for the day. Above the clipboard is a clothbound dictionary, closed, also ready, grimed and frayed. Beside the dictionary, a pocket thesaurus. To the left of the machine are an eraser, a type-cleaning brush, a beer can opener, an ashtray that I never use, seven assorted books—one *The Canterbury Tales*—and the cold cup of coffee which I shall drink within the hour.

It is secure here. Today is my day; perhaps, I might do something worthwhile today. But how many mornings and nights have I sat eating breakfast, dinner, sandwiches and coffee, drinking beer, wine, whiskey and cola, scribbling letters to nearly forgotten friends, relatives and loved ones, reading envied favorites, regretting, despairing, waiting to begin? How many have I spent? Straining back the sloth and fatigue, getting back to the string of ideas let go the night before or cursing, scolding, crying secretly to snatch it up again.

There is but one question and that is why I await each morning to try to write or watch it pass with bitterness, with hate, without making a mark upon paper, passing as a signal that the death of one added sun and moon nears my work to its final completion, though there is little upon paper as testimony of the passing. Why do I eagerly, but with dread, await these mornings, cursing the evenings my fingers are clumsied by doubt, my mind fogged by drink, drugs or the lust for a woman who is late? Each day without working is surrender to death. Sixty I see myself, sixty with nothing upon the paper, the pages all blank, as empty as a life without smudges. What will I have for it then? Blank pages? A life spent in searching for that unknown something that is seldom found. Things better found between the lines upon blank pages?

And what if I write volumes, what then? At sixty, what if I can accept death with libraries of song, score upon score of verse, left in my wake, spreading their ripples across the consciousness of the race. Will it be worth it then? Worth it to who? Will these mornings have been well-spent? Will the dream evenings matter which preface my days, the lonely nights away from light and laughter? Away from a woman who cannot reason why one must lock himself in dim rooms, hosting books, cold coffee, typewriter and thousands of blank sheets of paper. A desert, a void representing nothing. Empty blank pages. A woman who sees only the filled pages, pages filled in the darkness, the sadness, as nothing but paper. A woman who never understands how I feel about the pages, all the pages I can never fill. Is it worth it to be? Is it worth the living to continue . . . worth even the thinking that there is anything to continue . . .

The Real Me

Well, yeah, the name is Jess Brown, but don't print that—I don't dig it. Just call me Jaye Bourvier III.

So, you want to interview me 'cause I'm an authority on the "New Breed." Well, ya know, bein' a member doesn't immediately make me an expert—ya know—I mean it does sort'a put me on the inside, if ya know what I mean. But, anyway, I've made some scenes, ya know, and . . . what? Well, ya know, bein' one of those cats. Gettin' sucked into the group and bein' for real . . . yeah, I was serious about it. God! . . . was I serious. But I became hip; see? I saw it was to my advantage. No, man . . . it's like this. I am a professional Negro. Well, no, I don't mean I'm like a doctor or teacher or any of that bourgeois noise. To put it frankly: I make my problem pay—yeah—I'm in it for what I can get. Wait, man, I'm not puttin' you on. Don't you get it? There's all kinds of benefits in bein' a member of a minority these days. I mean, with all things considered, the field is opening up more and more . . . ya know—bein' black and meanin' it. We're in vogue these days, and think of it; realistic, I mean, it isn't so hard as it seems to qualify, and besides we're likeable . . . I even dig some Negroes myself—my mother's one.

Okay . . . well, this is how I got in this groove. What? No, I don't feel guilty or anything for takin' advantage of the situation. For a while I was square—ya know—sincere, I mean, and really honest about the whole thing. Like, I used to ask myself, "Is this what I really want?" No, man, not bein' born black; not bein' a Negro even; bein' in the group, I mean.

Before—ya know—I remembered how, when I was a kid, how I felt bad, at times, for bein' born black; not exactly resentin' it—ya know—but wondering: "Why does it have to be me?"

Well, I started searchin' for my identity . . . "Yeah" . . . I said . . . "that's what I'll do—find myself." So, these past two years, I've made the whole trip and I know what all this "New Negro" jazz is about. I really know the scene 'cause I've really made the break from the group and become an individual, see? I can look at the real picture objectively. I'm really me now. Yeah, you can say I'm a bit opportunistic now; but, hell, we individualists are like that.

Before, I had to be something—ya know—you had to be on the in to be in the group, see? But you had to be more hip to what was in to really be in, see? Everything was a front—ya know—everything a shuck. Man, you had to dress continental when continental was in style and drive a "Bird" or imported make . . . and well, I can go on and on . . . but you have to give some of those people credit. They're sick . . . wow! . . . but are they serious, and I can't stand sincerity. After all the phoneys I've met . . . whew . . . I'm glad to be myself again; I'm in my groove now. I'm proud of my heritage; I'm completely adjusted. Er . . . yeah, you spell Bourvier with an r.

The Drive

After a Friday night shift, he had gotten off work on a hot August morning, eaten a greasy breakfast in the employee's cafeteria, and decided to take a drive. He headed back through town by freeway, from East L.A., and then took the off-ramp at San Pedro Street and headed south. As the sun rose and the whiffs of smog and exhaust fumes fanned over the streets, the road's slick surface shot up heat waves bouncing before him, inviting him to follow them to the ocean. The drive to Long Beach was grueling without the sea breezes he searched after. A swing through the main carnival-like street, crowded before noon by sailors at hot dog stands, gave him nothing to park for, so he drove farther south, out along the beach, looking on houses painted pastel, opening their orchid, scarlet and blue doors on blazing beaches.

In early afternoon he turned back to Los Angeles and chanced on a freeway and zoomed for miles not knowing where he'd end up, but reached center city after finding out he had been on the Harbor Freeway. He still didn't want to go home, so got off far past his exit at Civic Center and headed west again, then south. Farther on, he turned on Adams Boulevard and pointed his old Ford toward the ocean on the western border of the city. He passed Western Avenue and Crenshaw Boulevard, and the neighborhood became more Negro. He lived close to Vermont, below Adams, in a large rooming house, and the western side of L.A. was almost unknown to him, as was most of the southern. He drove on, changing direction, heading north and then west and then north and again west, driving along Venice Boulevard and finally Santa Monica. He continued until he reached the ocean.

He had been to Santa Monica once before, on a chill and deserted autumn afternoon when he took an old girlfriend and her kid down there, nearly a year before. But this time instead of stopping the car in the huge, empty public parking lot and looking for hours out to sea with rock 'n roll drumming from the radio and salt spray pecking at the windows and gulls veering above and out seaward into the cold gusts, while he sipped beer and caressed a girl's breasts and thighs as her kid snored in the backseat, he got out of the car after parking it and walked down the beach front, down past Pacific Ocean Park (POP), scorching, loud and raucous, not shut and waiting for spring and weekends like before.

He walked, seeing the beach front change from the gaudy show of amusement park to dilapidated tenements, aged hotels and store fronts for osteopaths, faith healers, Jewish recreation centers and bars. The crowd changed like the neighborhood. Old European-style Jews appeared on the benches and crept along the walk ahead of him or crowded around the open-air fruit stalls, feeling the tomatoes.

They looked as if they had been lifted from an East Side New York street and set down blocks south of Santa Monica to wait for eternity in the California sun, beside a picture postcard sea.

Close to Venice West he stopped in a beer bar, the pounding jukebox guiding him. It was a gay joint, but he was thirsty, so he stayed and ordered a pitcher of beer. Two male couples sat at different ends of the bar, their made-up eyes roving and suspicious at first, until turning back to their matters. Behind the bar lounged a bull dike, wearing Levi's and button-down sports shirt, her hair in a duck-tail; she gabbed casually with him and didn't treat him as an intruder.

"You new in Venice?"

"Nawh . . . just drove down to try and get some air."

"Yeah . . . it's pretty hot . . . 'specially this time of year . . . I asked if you were new 'cause a lot of the Negro fellahs are movin' down here from the city and they make good customers. They're not square . . . ya know what I mean?"

"Yeah, I guess I do."

"The way I see it . . . a guy should do what he wants, ya know what I mean?"

"Yeah . . . yeah."

"Yeah . . . I keep a cool place. Everybody minds his business. That's the way it should always be . . . nice and cool."

They talked as he drank and the fags played the jukebox, and the bartender and he learned that they had both visited the same out-of-the-way place in Spain, and by the time he went off into the unbearable afternoon, he admitted secretly that queers and dikes weren't so bad, if they knew where you stood.

Driving back to Los Angeles from the beach he stopped at a bar on Washington Boulevard. It had just opened for the day and the big owner, formerly a heavy-weight fighter, was talking to his slim bartender. There was only one other customer when he arrived.

He ordered gin and lemon, for the heat was bothering him on his trip back, and he had drunk three or four when two girls walked in. Both had nice builds. The darker one had a perfect behind flaring under her skirt, but her brown talkative partner had the sleek, stream-lined build that works out so well, sometimes.

The girls ordered rounds and talked to the bartender a while, and when ordering drinks again, sent one down to him. He was sitting two seats away, and after the next drinks which he paid for, the girls asked him over, and believing that he might be especially appealing that one day, he moved between them. The brown girl kept up a rapid dialogue of nonsense and he could see she was hitting on him, as much as his fogged gaze could see, but it was the black one with big soft eyes he wanted to make time with. But she let her partner do all the chattering which she did for three drinks or more; then she offered to sleep with him for fifteen bucks, her buddy thrown in for twenty-five, or twenty-five for either of them the entire day. ("You can keep time on *your* watch, ho-ney.")

It wasn't the thing of their being whores that depressed him; he'd bought some and sold some before, he mused; it was because he hadn't spotted them when they stepped through the door that made him uneasy. It made him unsure of himself.

They looked to him like a couple of the girls he had gone to college with over the past year since he had put down knocking around the country. They just looked so nice and wholesome like little office girls out on a fling, drinking their weekend away, or young married broads who got lonesome in the afternoons while their husbands worked. He gulped down a drink when he thought of that old stereotyped prostitute plying her goodies in the corners of his imagination and memory, the kind he hadn't seen since the service who still must exist in some seaport towns in the States, right out of yesterday. He felt like such a chump for playing Square John; he felt so uncool.

After that the drinks didn't seem to matter, and the girls left sometime later, and when the two went prowling out in the heat in their delicate summer frocks, the chirping of their throaty giggles in the air, he drank the cool drinks faster, and awoke that evening on a hospital slab, two harness bulls standing over him, asking him how much had he drunk before smashing his old Ford into their cruiser.

He Couldn't Say Sex

He couldn't say sex and he wondered why. Ten years he wondered, fearing to tell himself he didn't fear to say it—not even to the God he knew that wasn't.

"If I ever hear you say that nasty filth, boy, under this roof again, I'll give you a lesson you'll never forget," his mother said.

But the word oozed off syrupy July pavements filling his muggy playstreets in asphalt-thick waves. The word was scrawled indelibly across his ghetto-sooted mind; its imagery sloughed off his broiled black sheen in cascades of lust. The word settled in the depths of his hard quick haunches and tight thighs.

Twelve years he spent in alleyways, meeting where gutters congregate, in hungered ravaged backlots, filling out into the craven beast he was named. His music was street sounds:

"Gnash teeth and yowl, cat; knot fist and slash, man."

They say he's rhythmic; it's a fact he's black, sweat funky; it was seeping through swinging doors of taverns as he lay peering under to glimpse flashes of the whores' thighs as they squatted across the bar stools.

The word drifted down midnight hallways of tenements, finding him awake in frigid beds envying the couples clawing in the stairwells. It surmounted the whimpered snores of his pregnant, husbandless sister on the first night he cried from fear of his drenched belly. The word mingled with the strained grunts and coughs of his mother and his latest "uncle" in their closed door revelry.

"Sex, sex, sex!" punched at him. He smelled it; he dreamt it; he lived through its discovering paradoxes each moment of his twelfth year. The approach of each long night brought monstrous secrets to him from his black isolated bed.

"Where did you hear that word?" his mother asked.

They seldom directly answered each other.

"Is something wrong with it?"

"Don't you ever bring that word into this house again, boy, as long as you live under this roof."

And he never did: not under her roof nor beneath the heavens of the world for many years. He refused to say it aloud, but was twisted into a spiritual gnome with each guilty scream of the word from the unquieted pockets of his brain.

Not even in the following summer heat time did he allow the word to crawl across his tongue. Not ever again as a young lean animal (the last of his cat child days).

It struck him dumb with Doris in their first greasy discovering together. Not with Marie, nor with Reba, nor with Dot in all his rapine pawing did he betray himself. Not eons later in Sicily, nor Genoa, nor Port-au-Prince.

Certainly, he spoke other words: disreputable ancient Anglo-Saxon and Sicilian epithets learned in the gutters of Naples where he lay for so long aging and sodden.

He parroted all manner of family vilifications spoken in hip salty, funky cadences.

"Yeah . . . Actioncity . . . all you whoremongering bastards springing from my sweet sweet juices."

A thousand ports he anchored: clap, brig, and France, but no whisper from his lips of the accursed scourge.

"Why, Mother?" he once asked. "Why should I grow up stunted and phobic? Why should *don't* be my creed, because it's yours? Don't say God, you say. Don't be immoral. Don't; no, never question—well— What was my father like?"

"There's nothing you would want to hear 'bout your father that I can tell you, boy," was her reply.

And she remained mum. He wondered, "Why? Why? It's about *why* that I want to know. Damn the rest!—give me the mystery of why!"

He made himself an exile searching for truth, the whole big deal about the mighty why.

But why should he suffer from gnawing suspicions after the physical contact of the lay is over? Should he have forgotten it at once and flushed it all down the john or wrapped it in the soiled sheets awaiting the laundry truck? Can he ever flush away part of his Self with the spent sperm and leave the residue of his testosterone to the ministrations of detergents with only a shrug? Does he wish not to be reminded that it is he riding down the drain, his droppings being bleached snowy wonderful? Can he bleach away his desires in the catharsis of drink, drugs, confession, or the bed until sterile as the laundered bedding?

Circumcision and condoms were unmentionable secrets fit only for the trash can in his former dwelling. It took eighteen years and a crib experience in Colon to find the mystery of the hot water bottle hidden in the bottom of his mother's dresser drawer.

His mother still remains mum (sister has five bastards now).

He must punish girls of twenty, today, by banishing them from his bed before taking them in hand and demonstrating the practicalities of the hot water gadget.

"It isn't your fault, honey," he explains to all as his ingrained repugnance rises in his nostrils as the manipulation of the bag, the hose, and nozzle are taught.

His mother's church banished him (there was no place for a questioner). He raged through adolescence and young manhood in futile quests. Dozen upon dozen of conquests fell under his hammering charges on muslin counterpanes and still he wondered whether it was being done correctly. His fear of inadequacy was cruel.

How many bastards did he need to make himself a man? How many sleepless nights in strange beds spent probing for a Self that didn't make him puke did he need?

"Are you lying, bed-mates, when you swear I'm good, good, good?" he begs.

"Do you mean I'm as good as your husband? Better!" he questions them all.

He fled to France to learn the how of it—how ignorant he found he was.

What made him go through this hell? Was it his mother? Where was his father; he couldn't imitate his mother.

"Don't ever say that word. We don't act like animals in this family. Don't say it . . . good people don't have dirty thoughts . . . you dirty boy!"

He listened and feared. Fearing all the rubby dub porkies in the world when they screamed "Don't!"

Two hundred faces (and lots more) have grimaced

up at him from the sheets (and he feared everyone). Two hundred mouths pulled apart in mocking, leering, whiny, blathering nothingness: love, torture, hate ("I hate you, darling, for what you are and what you make me when I'm with you . . . and I would have it no other way"). Two hundred deadpanned, multi-hued expressions that promised ecstacy and manhood; lied of shame and pride; secured by barter, begging, rape and sodomy.

Two hundred nights and days he feared: Philly, Nice, Venice, Providence, Coco Solo. Two hundred gin-soured, perfumed pepperminted, garlicked breaths, and twice as many pressing breasts. Two hundred lies and ejaculations. Four trips to the man with the needle, nine bastards scattered in the mainstreams (with unsuspecting fathers, he hopes).

Fifteen years 3,000 miles away from mother, home and church, and he'll not return, for he is abandoned. Three million drunks, four loves, and five centuries wondering if three hundred have been made.

Bug-house bait, jail-house prone, slum-seeking, woman-hating, wife-deceiving, respectability-faking, cynic sneering, paranoic (passive aggressive)—*an all-American black boy*—guilt-ridden, but now vocal.

Now, good and goddamned vocal: loud and hard with teeth gritted vocal. Funky from the diaphragm vocal. Not believing nor caring what it means anymore vocal—for he never found the *why*.

"Sex, Mother," he says (Does it make you cringe? Burn a candle for him).

"Sex, Daddy. Was it good to you, Pops?" he mourns farewell (and whoever you were, do you still remember what it was like?).

"Sex, God," he curses (go sex yourself), and that goes for the whole shot.

"Sex, sex, sex, sex, America," he roars from his manure pile (with your millions of sexless wonders).

THE RALLY or
Dialect Determinism

Dark eyes shift upon batting bloodshot eyeballs, set in a black face, peering through the narrow door slot. The eyes squint into the darkness where a man stands, and the face pushes nearer the opening, barring the yellowed glare from within. From outside, streetlamps shine against the watcher's irises, as the splinter streaks of white glow like candle flickers in the widening pupils.

"Good evening," the visitor says.

With the door's crack, light scatters the blackness where the figure stands, in a bright rectangle with two shadowy forms bordered by its dark edges.

The door slams behind the man, shooting a whiff of chill air against the nape of his neck.

"Evening, brother!" the guard says as he shoves the man against a wall. The new arrival is shown how to stretch forward, fingertips touching the wall, legs wide apart, body canted with the shoes two feet away from the baseboard; his head, not to sag upon the wall, sits upon a tired neck, straining to center itself between feet and fingers.

"First time here?" the guard questions.

The man nods, bumping his forehead.

"If you'll just let me—" the man is frisked efficiently by dark busy fingers sliding along his arms and under his coat, briefly beside his crotch and down his legs to crunch and mangle his cuffs.

"Will you please empty your pockets out on that table?" The guard points to a kitchen-size brown table; a large picture of a serene brown man holds most of the wall space above the table. The word PEACE is painted in black letters around the room.

"Now, I'll have to take these things," the guard says, sliding the visitor's wallet, cards, currency and pictures into a numbered box. "You'll get these back right after the meeting."

"How?"

"Because you are number one," the guard says. "Inside, brother," he points down the corridor.

A dim hallway, painted light green, leads to an auditorium. Twin black runners leading to a wide, dark-green room meet at the foot of a podium. The room is filled, and a gross speaker stands upon the platform under a huge picture of the serene man. The word is painted upon the walls, ceiling and floor in this room. It is written upon the seat and back of every chair.

Men and women sit upright in folding chairs. There is a predominance of green business suits and chic shifts with exotic patterns. Birds rustle through purple foliage, across dark shoulders, with grape leaves mottling azure and scarlet backgrounds. Many of the men's ties are orange and slice down the fronts of their grey shirts.

"I call you brothers for we have a common experience," the heavy speaker croons, "and we will share a common future, for we have common aspirations and common destinies . . . as I've mentioned, so if our fates are shared, then we form a brotherhood, or for those of you who shun the unpleasantness you may find in this word, brotherhood, we will only say that we are here for mutual benefits . . . brothers . . . ha ha ha."

His movements are slow and flashy. A large white handkerchief is used to dab at his puffy lips and mop his forehead; he waves it like a banner whenever the crowd becomes excited.

"You see it doesn't hurt," he continues, "to be identified with your own. I mean . . . it's not half as bad as some of you newer ones might suspect." His oval eyes follow the new arrival until he takes a seat near the center of the room.

"TELL US ABOUT IT, BROTHER, TALK ABOUT IT," a large brown youth in front shouts.

"Yeah, bring it down front, man," other voices rise.

"Yaasss . . ." the speaker answers. He draws out the sound of affirmation when he is pleased by his audience. "I see what you mean," he says.

"GIVE US THE WORD," the youth shouts.

"Yes, the word!" is echoed throughout the hall.

Large eyes fix upon the newcomer from the front of the room; the speaker smiles while saying: "Well, you know that nationalism ain't an invention of brother . . . oh, sorry, I mean of the black man . . ."

"WHAT YAWHL SAY?" someone yells.

"Let brother speak!" someone says.

"It was with the rise of the European nation-state that nationalism becomes evident in history . . ."

"That's right!" the young man says.

"It is," a girl joins in. "Can't you hear those big words he's using; he's got to be right."

"Right!" someone yells.

The big man flutters his handkerchief.

"THAT'S RIGHT!" the young man shouts.

"Right!"

"Sho nuf!"

The crowd sways with the wonder of the speaker; it is an inner rhythm rushing up to their heads from their stirring seats, to burst out in explosive enthusiasm. Sitting still, the new man pulls his eyes away from the speaker's and focuses upon his feet, but his ears swim in the room's sound.

"Now in unity we have found by looking at history there is strength . . . in brotherhood there is power, and all we want is power, don't we, just like everybody else? . . . So as the most honest people on the face of the earth we don't have to fool ourselves by sayin' it's some sort of holy crusade or just fairness if we get our chance finally to kick the hell out of somebody else for a change . . ."

"Teach, brother," a voice shouts.

"THAT'S RIGHT!"

"Right! . . . we's de most honest folks . . . history proves dat," one of the audience yells.

"Now, brothers, are we really honest?" the speaker says, and before he is answered: "No, we are no more honest than other humans, for dishonesty is a human trait; ain't it, and ain't we human?"

"THAT'S RIGHT! THAT'S RIGHT! WE'S HUMAN, AIN'T WE!" a shout goes up.

"Teach, teach, teach, brother."

With the white handkerchief at his forehead, the large man stares out into the dim room as the new man raises his eyes from the floor and sees the fat shriveling from the heavy man's frame and the dark suit dissolve into musty brown tones. Whiffs of dead bones and skins waft through the skylight above the stage.

"The reason we don't have to worry about honesty is because this ain't our society no way and what's ain't yours you don't have ta care 'bout no way . . ." the speaker continues.

"THAT'S RIGHT! THAT'S RIGHT! WHAT WE'S HERE FO' IS TA GET THE FACTS, THE TRUTH AND NOTHIN' BUT!" the young man is standing upon his chair exhorting the speaker.

"Shut up, man, and let him talk!" someone yells.

"Yeah, let us hear the word," another joins in.

The eyes of the speaker point into the crowd; the youth takes his seat, and all eyes join to those two points in the universe except for the new man who trembles from his chair, his hands clamped against the bright scene on stage.

"Now let me tell you something you might not have guessed before," the speaker says. "You might not have known it but dis ain't America in the sixties . . ."

"What you say, brother," the dark youth yells, jumping from his seat.

"YOU WANTED THE TRUTH, SO I'M TELLING YOU THAT DIS AIN'T AMERICA YOU'S IN . . . RIGHT! . . ." the speaker shouts.

"That's what you said," another voice in the audience yells, "that's what you said, brother!"

"Yaasss . . ." the speaker continues, "now this is really Germany . . . the Germany of the late twenties and thirties . . . right?"

"Nawh, brother, nawh, man, we ain't gonna go fo' dat," the young man shouts.

"But, brother, you wanted the truth, so I am confessing that I'm Hitler . . . right!"

"NO! NO! WE AIN'T GOIN' FO' DAT!"

"Ain't I's Hitler?" the speaker challenges.

"No, yawhl not no Hitler."

"Maybe he's telling the truth," someone says. "I always wondered what happened to Hitler."

"Yawhl jivin' . . . yawhl shuckin'," the stranger hollers. He jumps from his seat and fastens his eyes onto the speaker's.

With a sweep of his hand the little mustached man on the platform smashes him back into his seat.

"And I told everyone I had a book coming out," the speaker continues. "You don't know whether I have a book coming out . . . right?"

"RIGHT!" two hundred voices scream.

"SING RIGHT!" the speaker's voice rings out.

"RIGHT!"

"Sho nuf!"

The visitor begins to whimper and tremble, but his sounds are ignored by the crowd.

"Ha ha ha . . . but, comrades, I am really Marx . . . right?" the speaker says.

"Wrong!"

"SING RIGHT!!!"

"WRONG!!!"

"YAWHL RIGHT, BROTHERS . . . ha ha ha . . . for I don't really knows that dere are only nine card-carryin' members in the L.A. cell . . . do I's . . . or are dere ten . . . or two hundred and fifty-eight." A haze surrounds the speaker as his voice whines, and the frightened man sees the form on stage wax and flow behind the voice.

"YAWL HEAR DAT . . . HE'S ONE OF DEM REDS," the youth shouts, pointing his finger to the dark mass.

"WOULDN'T YAWHL RATHER BE A FIRST-CLASS COMMUNIST THAN A SECOND-CLASS CITIZEN?" the speaker shouts.

"Nawh."

"Yeah, man."

"He said first-class," a flurry of voices.

"I don't want to be no mahthafukkin' Communist . . . I's a good American," the dark boy in front says.

"Shut up, Tom," someone shouts.

"Don't intimidate the young man . . . and get ahold of yourselves, folks . . . 'cause I got news for you," the speaker grins. "Now what's our password?"

"ILLOGIC!" rings out in the hall.

"YAASSS . . . CHILDREN . . . and for dat I'll confess dat I'm really an imposter . . . I's really Malcolm X . . . BLOODS . . . ha ha ha . . . yawhl." The speaker removes his horn-rimmed glasses and wipes his shaven head with the handkerchief.

"THAT'S AN OUTRIGHT SLANDEROUS LIE PUT IN YOUR MOUTH BY WHITE DEVILS," a tall brown man in black suit and red tie shouts; he is the exact copy of the tall brown man in glasses standing upon the platform. "I'M MALCOLM X!" the strange man screams and starts toward the platform.

"Shut him up," the brown youth hollers. "I should know Malcolm when I's see him and dat don't look no nothin' like him."

There is a scuffle with ten men milling around the tall man taking their karate stances. The loud youth balls up his fist and rushes up to the man and shakes it in his face just out of reach.

"I's a killer, a mangler, a mad dog when I's gets started. I's so bad I's have to hold myself back; you better be careful, boy!" the youth repeats thirty times.

The fight begins when the boy pushes one of his gang within the reach of the waiting man who breaks the tough's neck, collarbone and hipbone with a nifty judo chop, and the mob break out of their defensive poises to save their fallen brother.

"Liar."

"Peace, brother."

"Fraud."

"Take dat, brother."

"Mahthafukker."

"Teach da truth, man."

The tall man is finally wrestled out of the hall by twenty-five men, as the brown youth shakes his fist at their exit and informs the crowd: "He better not come back or I'll whup him so bad his mama won't take him in."

"I'm glad that cowardly dog is gone," the speaker says, his beribboned uniform sparkling in the quieting hall. "To attempt to smear my good name . . . the idea."

Hushes are called for among the crowd.

"See," the speaker says, "now that order has been gotten at the expense of a few, I can say positively that I am Lenin, right, for he came before Stalin, so I am my own Second Coming."

"Wowee . . . listen to him . . . he knows everybody," the youth cries.

"Then he must be everybody," someone answers.

The visitor moans and many heads turn.

"Hush yo mouf," a black young lady stands and orders the speaker.

"But, sister," the speaker says, "ain't you never seen me befo . . . ?" He explodes before the visitor in a nova.

"Nawh . . . I ain't never seen no nothin' like you before," the lady challenges.

The visitor sees the flashing particles draw together and fuse into a single entity.

"Well, I've been away for quite some time, honey," the voice on stage says, "I's really the Wandering Jew."

"The wandering who?" it is asked.

The beam drifts and glides about the stage, skirting the edges of the stage apron and then whirling backwards to slide through the cracks in the stage floor like smoke. "Don't yawhl knows I's Martin Luther, Butterbeans without Susie," the voice resounds. "That I's Uncle Tom, Fred Schwarz, Emperor Goldwater, Lumumba, Castro, all the L.B.J.'s, Lincoln Rockwell, the Birds' Turds resurrected . . . chickenshit, ya hip?"

"Teach, brother."

"That's right!"

"Sho nuf . . . dat's where it's at."

"And in all my glory I's de greatest," the speaker shouts.

"THAT'S RIGHT!" the brown youth in front screams and staggers.

"Teach, brother . . . speak the word, the word, the word," the crowd repeats.

The visitor bites his lip and chokes.

"Very well," the speaker answers, "I'll give you more, everything and whatever you wish to hear."

"Give it to us, brother."

"Teach . . . teach . . . teach, brother!"

"The word, the word, the word!"

With great eyes formed, the cloud takes shape as a

black presence. The voice beats out as though it comes from everywhere in the room; the stranger can almost see the lips of the serene picture move: "I'S DE GREATEST . . . I'S DE ONE AND ONLY WHO WILL TELL YAWHL DAT WHOEVER SELLS HIS SOUL FOR POWER MUST COME TO ME, THE POWER-GIVER . . . THE SINGLE VOICE WHO WILL HIP YOU TO THIS, BROTHERS: THERE'S A MESSIAH ON EVERY CORNER! AND WE'RE ALL OUT HERE TO FUCK YOU . . . BROTHERS . . . !"

"THE TRUTH! THE FINAL TRUTH!" the youth throws back his head and wails.

"*Aaaa wooo ouwwalll weeesss wa booogie* blues in de alley soul so much soul so soulful, lawdy, yes indeedy, yawhl," a fat girl goes into a trance.

"Now, yawhl knows dat I's goin' ta take ov'va, so let me tell ya how's I's goin' ta do it so you can help me out," the speaker says and his fat shape waddles to the blackboard. The slit of his suit coat is pushed out by his high pockets, and his pants fall below his sloping stomach, a wrinkled bunching in the crotch.

Reaching for the chalk, the speaker writes DIALECT DETERMINISM . . . YAWHL!

There are rustles in the audience and grunts of cleared throats mixed with the squawks of parrots and farts of zebras. The speaker turns and smiles.

"Dialect . . . what's dat?" voices whisper.

"Ummuummm . . . ?"

"REMEMBER THOSE WORDS, BROTHERS," the speaker shouts.

"We'll remember!" most voices answer.

"Now, to bind us closer together," the speaker continues, "we needs a martyr."

"YEAH, DAT'S WHAT WE NEEDS IS A MARTYR," the brown youth hollers.

"Say, what's dat?" someone asks.

Eyes search throughout the room, under seats, in pockets and purses, to the visitor drying his eyes; he shakes his head and stares toward the front of the hall. The speaker sees all eyes upon himself.

"RIGHT!" the speaker says.

"Right!" the audience repeats, rising as one except for the stranger.

"SING RIGHT!!!" the speaker screams with the laying on of all hands.

"RIGHT!!!" The mob surge up on stage, their fingers tearing away his clothes. He smiles at the visitor as he is trampled among his brothers.

"I'll get the rope," the brown youth says and bounds from the stage, running up the aisle past the visitor who is nearing the door.

A rope is dragged from a broom closet in the hallway and the brown youth almost knocks the strange man over as he returns to the auditorium.

At the door, the guard hands the visitor his personal items. They shake hands. The portrait of the serene man glistens in the soft light; its eyes cast upon the entire scene.

"Come again, brother," the guard says.

"I'll try."

He is helped into his coat; a rallying cheer arises from the auditorium.

"Never seen my people in such high spirits," the guard says. "Well, goodnight, brother, Peace be with you."

"And Peace remain with you, brother," the visitor says, pulling away from the warm eyes, and stepping through the doorway.

The Messenger

"Ah mumble mumble mumble . . . Ah mumble mumble mumble . . ."

Early, with the first light, came Rick's morning prayer from his room. Rick gave vows to his black god. He had no time to present the other four chants his faith demanded during the day and evening, for his one dawn devotional cost him precious time spent upon his knees, time necessary to his cause. Being unorthodox, as he called himself, he said he was free to interpret his new faith in an individual way.

That's all it is, brothers, that's all it is . . . a shuck, just a shuck to stay on your knees prayin' all the time for things to change and not gettin' out there and doin' somethin' 'bout 'em. The devil's not on his knees! . . . No, the devil's not jivin' . . . not one hundreth of the time that brother is . . . the devil gave brother religion for one purpose . . . to take the chains from his wrists and put them around his mind!

The paint on my window frame and baseboard and upon the walls in all the rooms of the house was a combination battleship grey and flesh pink. When we moved in, the landlady, Mrs. Goodstein, offered it to hide the blotched walls; it had been bought at a war surplus store.

After Mrs. Goodstein had left, Rick, with paint cans obstructing his path, had paced the length of the long living room, tirading against all "Anns" (as he called white women). And he denounced every woman—black and white—engaging in commerce and business—not solely in domestic duties.

"Ah mumble mumble mumble . . . Ah mumble mumble mumble . . ."

It had been a bad day for Len and me.

I sat in a corner reading book reviews, passing the pages to Len as I became offended by the critics. Len and I whispered little and strained to hear the FM above Rick's teachings, hoping that he would not accidentally tilt a can upon the nearly large enough, patched and sewn, once maroon rug.

Rick's narrow, highly polished black shoes scampered like ebony shrews among the gallons of grey and flesh, always just skimming past the containers, over the half-dozen glass quarts of turpentine, above the faded, no longer imperial, floor covering. Even when the toes, from the outset of a reckless swoop, were sweeping to a collision to smashing vivid spangles upon the carpeting, they somehow slid past, carrying their messenger upon his path of righteousness.

"Ah mumble mumble mumble . . . ah mum mum mum . . ."

Rick finished praying; the floor's creak disclosed him getting from his knees in the center of the room. With routine rigid as his backbone, he stretched first, then puffed out his chest, for he had done his duty. Next he strode to the FM and CLICK; it was on . . . so morning had fully come.

"JIVIN' JONES! JIVIN' JONES . . . THE HIP ONE!" Rick screamed.

Each weekday morning was like the last; Rick up

first and the Jiving Joe Jones Rhythm 'N Blues Program turned on. But Rick hated blues.

"Get up, brother Steve," he spoke to me. "Get brother Len up too so he can listen to Jivin' Jones's message."

I saw his gossamer form through my web of curtain, spinning away from my doorway, his shaven gleaming skull seeming like a haloed globe through the curtain, approaching Len's shut door on the far end of the couch; each morning Rick awoke the world to his screams.

"Yes, brothers . . . get up, get up for dancing and singing . . . ha ha ha . . . get up for playin', brothers; we all know what great players black men are . . . yawhl. Listen to Jivin' Jones, brothers, ain't he hip? AIN'T HE HIP? Wants you to dance your life away. JIVIN' JONES! Black people have got more records than books . . . YEAH! . . . Dance your lives away!"

Then Rick was at the hi-fi turning the volume higher; he raised his chant above the blast, and the shuffle of his slim shoes gave me the image of him gyrating across the floor, burlesquing the latest dance steps, eyes shut tight against light in imitation bliss, body whirling, buttocks protruding, absurdly jutting beneath the flaps of his slit suit coat.

"JIVIN' JONES WILL TELL YOU ALL YOU NEED TO KNOW; LISTEN TO HIS MESSAGE, BROTHERS!"

"*As-salaam alaikum*, brother Steve," Rick said as I stepped into the living room, barechested, hands filled with shirt, shoes and towel.

He sat at one of the two tables in the room, writing in an old looseleaf tablet.

"Morning, Rick."

Beyond the living room was Len's bedroom. To enter

the bathroom off the tiny chamber, I shoved the door against his yielding mattress, and slid my body through the opening. As I jerked through, my twisted head looked down upon Len's bearded, slumbering face.

In the bathroom my face cloth still hung in its place. Some mornings it was gone or pushed and fallen into the tub it hung above.

I reentered the living room; Rick gathered up his books and materials.

"There're some English muffins in the oven, brother. I hope you don't mind an Anglicized breakfast, but English muffins don't have filthy pork grease in them. Yes, the Englishman is a heavy man. Did you know that, brother Steve?"

"I had guessed as much," I said and turned the fire up under the frying pan before spreading the few slices across the oily steel.

"You're still eating pork, I see."

Rick stood in the kitchen doorway, hands upon sides, distaste showing upon his light tan face.

"There's nothing I can say to break you of this filthy habit?" he asked.

"No."

"But to consume swine . . . to eat the nastiest scum-sucking, filth-swilling vermin in creation is nauseous, brother. A hog, a sow, a pig is dirty, brother Steve. It's devil food!"

Too much flame shriveled the strips, scorching their edges brownly in curls, raising glistening puffs of fat in the centers of the curls. Looking me over as I fished out the bitter scraps, Rick shrugged, then turned away.

"Oh well," he said. "Some of my brothers just aren't

ready yet." He returned to the kitchen doorway. "But we *need* you, brother. We need poets as well as builders." He turned once more, final and done.

He gathered up his books and adjusted his glasses; I wondered how he'd see once the downpour swept against the lenses. A clear plastic raincoat with ends spreading out like a kite was to keep him dry, and transparency revealed his black suit and stiffly starched white shirt. His books and pamphlets were wrapped in a plastic bag. A great black umbrella hung from his arm by its curved neck, and new, glossy black rubbers covered his wicked-looking sharp-toed shoes.

"Just think of the songs you could sing of your people in your poetry, Steve. The black man lives in song and poetry."

"If I could only sing truth, Rick, buddy, I'd be glad," I said.

"Isn't the black man truth, brother Steve?" he replied. "Isn't he fact; are you your own dark lie, or does the lie belong to the devil?"

I turned and stared at him; then I reached down into my saucer and picked up a charred strip of pork, biting through its tough fat, licking the grease from my smacking lips with relished swipes of tongue.

Rick lowered his head; the overhead light lit his stripped, skin-drawn skull; I saw the surface plainly, naked and tan.

"I have a meeting to attend all day, so I won't be back until this evening," he said.

I nodded, my mouth stuffed by breakfast.

"*As-salaam alaikum*, brother," he said, using the Arabic address, backing out the front door. Some storm spray plucked off his uncovered scalp and skewed down his brown brow in zagging streaks. He shook out his umbrella and closed the door.

See you later, prophet, I thought as the door shut, and reached over and snapped the blues nob to "off." Finally, I plunged into the kitchen and puked the pork into the sink.

PART TWO

THE
HUNGERED
ONE

The Hungered One

He suspected no unnaturalness in the flock. The pigeons were feeding upon salted nuts that some other passer-through had scattered down. He walked among the birds, tolerating the nearly tamed ones who grudgingly strutted from his path, hindering him on his tour.

His shoes crushed nuts, making his soles slip; he scraped them as he walked, startling the flock to leap briefly from the ground. It was during their resettling that he saw the strange one; it had remained aground, determined, pecking with its vicious beak, about its companions' flitting feet.

It was larger than the other birds, weighing as much as a kept duck, and was a pale blue shade. No feathers clothed it; its tinted skin looked scaly, thirsty, and hot. More important to the young man were the bird's four legs which sprouted from its muscular, squat body, grey and coarse. Black talons shielded its toes, and splintered dewclaws dangled from the backs of each leg.

The man gaped at the blue creature. The flock remained aloof, leaving it isolated, spinning counterclockwise like a dog, in an island of goobers, awkward, unable to lower its short neck completely to the ground. Its hooked beak came within a hair of the nuts, causing its labors to be of little profit, but fortunately, the bird

discovered occasional kernels lying upon small protu-
berances that jutted from the pocked, uneven ground.
Then it would snap them up with clicking sounds.

Most of the flock kept clear of this vortex of frenzy;
for the unfeathered one tore after its meal, a hundred
pecks to their one, although receiving only a hundredth
of their portion, and so furious were its random actions,
that at times, in the fury of filling its craw, it snapped
up careless birds which had gotten too near to it, and it
devoured them wholly.

The young man stood until twilight, observing the
movements of the creature. No other human passed that
way; night was an awaited arrival. Many of the feeders
took to wing, to soar in coveys, coated by the crimson
rays of sun. One by one, the birds rose to race in scores
about the treetops, until singly landing exhausted in
their nests, to chirp, fretful into sleep.

As night sulked down the green paths, there was still
enough light for the young man to fully distinguish the
bird, which seemed to feed more rapinely upon its feast.
The creature appeared to seize even fewer tidbits, almost none now, for its clicking beak erred when a mor-
sel came within reach, and it would bite into the crumb
instead of gobbling, resulting in the pieces falling from
the bird's beak as it adjusted its hold.

The young man became impatient and approached
the nut-gatherer. He knelt down and scooped up a hand-
ful of the nuts and offered them to the distressed one.
The naked thing fixed the interloper in its stare. Its eyes
were round and yellow, more suited for a snake's than a
bird's. The yellow orbs scrutinized the bits lying in his
extended hand, now easily within reach, and then the

bird flicked out its stubby neck; its cruel beak snatched at nourishment. It tore off the outer joint of the index finger from the young man's hand.

"Yeee . . ." filled the small glade. The victim sprang away and flapped his hand at the end of his sleeve; then he placed the stump in his mouth and sucked at the spurting blood, before taking out his handkerchief and wrapping his finger in a bandage.

The bird had resumed feeding. Light flared on, the swift pecker was revealed standing in shadows, whirling in its continuous circle.

After he had reduced the bleeding, the young man again returned to the creature. He crouched over it, waiting for it to skip away, but the thing stopped its spins and stared up at him. The gas lights glistened in the reflection of its eyes, and a luminous halo surrounded each iris when the man looked closer. He reached down and took the bird in his hands. With maimed finger extended, he gripped the thing's drumsticks; his thumbs and forefingers encircling the forelegs; his remaining fingers helping to brace the bird's hind legs and tail.

"I'm taking you home with me, strange fellow."

He began walking toward an exit; the creature roosted, tranquil, upon his knuckles; they reached the gate in minutes.

Night was dabbed with jasmine; it was a black interlude when crickets tuned their bows and mockingbirds pursued low melodies. The stars hung like trinkets against night's sordid veil.

A cab was waiting at the corner; its driver drew on his cigarette, shooing away the fireflies which sought to mate with the fiery glow.

"Can you take me home?" the young man said.

"That's my job, son."

"It's over on Dixon Street."

"Okay." The driver pushed open the door; the passenger light uncovered the weird cargo. "Christ! What's that?"

"I don't know . . . found it in the park."

"Well . . . just look at it . . . those eyes . . . Hey, what happened to your hand?"

"My friend bit part of my finger off."

"Hey . . . I don't know if I can take you. I don't carry dangerous animals."

"It's okay. He's quiet now and I've got him back here with me. He'll never bother you."

"Well . . . if you say so. But I should take you to a doc first. Animal bites are dangerous."

"Later. I want to get my little friend home safely."

The cab started. The silent bird turned its broad head toward the park which fell away through the rear window. It then fastened its eyes upon its captor and beat its false wings three swift times.

"How did you find him, buddy?" the cabbie said.

"Just walked up on him. I couldn't believe my eyes at first. God, I'm really lucky."

"You sure are . . . that thing will bring you a nice hunk of dough."

"Oh, I ain't gonna sell him."

"No? Then what's the good of it . . . what do you want a thing like that for?"

"I don't know. I just want to get him home right now and feed him. He looked so starved out there in the park."

The bird didn't change its gaze but lunged for the young man's mouth; its beak fell short of the tongue but dug a furrow down the chin and along the man's breastbone.

"Oww . . . dammit, he's started up again."

"Well . . . let him go, fellah, he's not worth it."

The blue creature was now jerking its legs, causing its restrainer to rearrange his hands. The wound bled freshly.

The driver braked to a halt and bolted from his door, reaching back and pulling open the rear.

"Quick, throw him the hell out. It ain't right to keep a thing like that."

"Please help me; I've got him."

"No; no, I won't touch that thing. Look how he's trying to reach down after your blood."

The creature was pecking, frustrated by its stump of a neck, at the young man's hands; it was unable to reach the wound but pecked the bandage several times, shredding it.

"Stop," the young man screamed, "I'll feed you when we get home. I'll feed you."

"It's a devil," the driver said.

The heavy bird wrestled one foreleg from the clutching hands and fastened its claws upon the young man's wrist. The claws gripped like tongs and dug in, immediately bringing blood, until the man's whole arm was slippery red. The creature swarmed over the man's fists, ripping spots from his palms which he now used to shove the bird from the door.

"It's horrible," the driver moaned. "Get rid of it."

"Help me," the young man cried.

With a lunge, the man forced the thing from him and out the cab's door. The terrible beast landed upon its back with its four legs kicking in the air. The driver swiped at it, hoping to stomp its head, but the featherless thing regained its legs and rushed its new assailant; the driver was routed, filling the blackness with quakes and babbles.

The berserk thing scurried back to the cab and leaped through the doorway; the young man was now upon his knees, with hands protecting his eyes, showering tears down his shirt front to converge with the rivulets of red. As the bird extended its neck to examine its prey, the man shot out his mangled hands and encircled the thing's throat and beat its head against the car's footrest. The creature kicked out with its many claws, attempting to disembowel its foe, but before the man fainted, he split the monster's head, exposing its brains. Finally, the blue thing wriggled out of the clamped fists, displaying a limp wing and a partial view of its inner skull. It didn't bleed; its eyes, still yellow and alert, stared at its host. Then it made one more move toward the unconscious human, to tear a strip from his thigh and turn, to hobble from the vehicle. It scrambled along the street, in the direction of the sleeping flock, looking like some huge rodent or totally diseased hen with a large worm in its beak. It was an earthbound thing which would never leap into the sky to circle the treetops, camouflaging its strange complexion against the backdrop of the heavens.

When the ambulance arrives, the young man has been taken by shock.

"I wonder what happened to the poor bastard?" a bystander questions.

"Who knows, probably a teen-aged gang," she is answered.

Inside the ambulance, the plasma is being rigged, and sedatives rush the young man into nightmares. The attendant asks him: "What happened, mister? What happened?"

"He was so hungered," the hurt man says. "I only wanted to take him home . . . to feed him . . . to feed him well."

The Saviour

They stand about his bed as his eyes open in the blackness, their fingers pressing into his arms, wedging them against his sides, the fingers clamping down his legs and feet. Into his mouth a gag is stuffed deep, and adhesive tape is pasted across his lips. The blindfold wrings his eyes, pressing them into their sockets to flash in aching novas. The floor they stand him upon is chill. He lifts one foot from the surface, but they jar him still. His tongue pushes behind the gag to keep the soggy lump from sliding into his throat, and his Adam's apple jerks as spit sloughs past his windpipe.

They shove him toward the door; he gauges the distance across the familiar room in wide steps, anticipating the footstool that they kick from the way. Outside, the winter mist covers his shoulders, but the hands upon him tighten as his tremors increase. Across frosted grass, ice crystals catch between his toes, with the graveled driveway pricky and filled by scuffing sounds from many boots. A car door opens and he is inside, the fingers only tightening. Growls of motor and chewing of gears and a soft acceleration; they jerk him upright; his head snaps, joggling his teeth. He groans as the fingers press.

They drive in darkness, a drive through winter night along naked roads. A good car. A well-made, comfortable machine with no other sound from motor or spinning parts than the tick from the dashboard clock. Springs excellent. Comfort. Smoothness and precision. Craftsmanship riding in blackness.

Spots glow and circle on the inner lids before his eyes. He strains to see into the blackness and the spots ignite in hues, and constellations spin like microscopic viruses through his blind brain. A lump of saliva passes down his throat, and he flares his nostrils in an extended breath. The fingers tighten and his own tingle while sparks tease the marrow of his limbs.

A cave. Once he was lost in a cave in Virginia. A big cave it was that he and a friend had found and slept in that night. In the morning he had walked far back into its interior, and had smashed his spotlight when he tripped into a subterranean gully. Just the blackness until he was found ten hours later. Blackness and sounds. Sounds of water dripping and small scurryings with tumbles of pebbles scratching down the sides of his trap. He sat and listened and strained eyes into blackness until he could make out the hues and far cosmos.

They drag him from his seat. The sand under feet is gritty. Waves are heard in front of his blindfold, and the frozen breath of the ocean flutters his pajamas. They turn him and walk more than a mile through sand and weeds. Shells dent his soles, and the fingers press whenever he stumbles upon a dune.

A panel slides open and warm air surrounds as they pass inside. Boots beat upon boards and his feet catch some splinters, but their progress isn't slowed until a door is opened and he is led inside a dank compartment.

They set him upon a stool; he feels its circular edges with the tips of his fingers. Their fingers release, but his hands are banged by a hard object when he tries to massage his arms. The fabrics of his holders' suits are smooth and tight; his fingernails rustle along the arm of one of them as he snatches his hand away. With a tear the adhesive is ripped from his lips, and the gag is jerked out bringing more skin.

"Hey," he shouts and someone smashes him in the mouth, toppling him backwards.

Hands grab him up and set him back in place; then the blindfold is taken off. It is black in the room. As he blinks, the hands and fingers fall away and the shift of shiny material and the stomp of boots clop to the door; it slams.

A gull preens by morning light, claws webbed, just short of white froth, swishing up to shore. South, sand trickles to fogbank, where figures stir, smoke rising about their legs, as black poles stretch seaward. From the north a bird sinks to the sand. Two stand, black-tipped beaks upon throats.

Figures emerge from mist, pass the fishermen, as sun reflects green in the swells which rise and speed to shore, collapsing spent white in foam.

Seven gulls stand pestering sand fleas among their tail feathers. Other birds descend; the covey numbers ten, then fifteen. Splashes bring peeps. Water sloshes across feet—shrieks sound as the outer circle pushes. Three birds skate on billows, dragging legs atop crests until the surge breaks streaming against the sand as the flyers veer up and swerve about. One wave spills over the flock. Squawks and trampled feathers, but calm settles; a few peck at beer cans, others shred gum wrappers. They all sweep to the sky.

Man and dog race over a dune; the man splashes to the surf, shouting, scolding the poodle to obey. A woman staggers after them. Waves smash; she screams, struggling to high ground. The man beckons with his back to the sea; water swamps him to the waist. Upon a rise the dog meets the couple where it has waited; the trio continues north, and there is laughter.

Birds soar above the shore and out to sea and in about the cliffs. Sun shows waves; the waves dark within, their depths indigo where shadows swim. Footprints and claw marks scatter among butts and shells. Gulls stream by until one spirals in and settles.

He is asleep when they slap him; his eyes pop open to see blackness, and then the blindfold covers. No gag. They jerk him to his feet and lead him through the door and turn. The walk is with fingers gripping, boot sounds and whirling brain lights. Another door opens. There is space. An awaiting. A reaching, then they descend steel stairs, the wide grilled patterns imprinting their cold forms upon his soles. Shakes and vibrations of boots tremble the metal structure, ringing jolts through his spine to brain and blending the shocks across his strapped eyeballs in dashes of pink waves.

Their feet reach bottom. Cement. Damp cement with the steel taps of the boots chinking, and his bruised insteps prancing across the cracks.

They stop. Wet blast of air follows the creak of giant hinges and they climb down deep, greasy stone steps. He slips but is caught by the fingers which shake him fully awake and with one step, they are at the end. Dirt, close packed with pebbled forms, is the floor.

Candlelight pierces his lids as his blindfold is pulled away. His hands reach for his face and halt and start once more, feeling no fingers. Slowly the candles soften until he sees.

Five sit ten feet in front of him behind a wide plank supported by twin sawhorses. They sit upon barrels, and they wear purple robes, black veils covering their faces, all nodding in turn. All wheedle by sign language, coax through gesture and mimic disturbance. All do not see him in the pressure of their activity.

He steps forward, but once again fingers gouge into his arms. His holders are in black; shiny black suits which expose their great chests, biceps and thighs. Red hoods cover their heads; oval holes are cut into the face pieces, with blackness behind the covering.

"But wha—" he begins and is punched in the face by a ringed fist. He teeters upon his knees staring at the black edges of their boots, but the candlelight is too faint to show him the redness which flows from his mouth and mangled nose.

Rows of green line the valley bed with crisscrossing silvery slashes of irrigation ditches. The valley is not seen from the highway running down the coast, but the intersecting dirt road hooks back behind the slope, and the old gully where water bubbles down to the shore in spring opens into the shallow expanse where the groves stand, the sun and ocean mist ripening their berries, keeping the fruit tenders occupied. None find time to circle the hill and discover the sea, and the sand remains for the prints of gulls.

He has been standing for more than two hours. The first time they kicked him they didn't knock all his wind out, but his pretending got him more. He awoke upon his feet, fastened by the fingers, facing the whispering men who went about their duties.

With a nod, the five robed men face front. And his blindfold is placed back by the fingers, but before the dark, he sees a veil quivering.

The fingers push him about and return him to his quarters. Inside, in the blackness, they remove his blind- fold. Their boots draw back, the door slams, and he is left blind in the blackness.

Boot sounds awake him later, the door swinging open, the feel of air currents flow and emptiness, and then a clank of something being placed beside his stool. Boot clicks leave with the door's slam, and the tap tap tap down the hallway through the blackness.

He reaches out and fingernail scrapes metal. A mug. Water. Through broken nose he sniffs the water; thirst has him gulp the cooling wetness, washing his dam- aged mouth clear of mucus and clots. His fingers find a pitcher. More water until his belly grumbles. And then he sleeps.

Boot noise brings food, and then water, and after there is sleep in darkness. His fingers become restless; they explore and discover a basin and cot. And then his toilet. One index finger blunders into the baseboard vent which supplies him with air, and is caught for minutes.

The blackness total, with the colored universes spiraling in orbits, pulsating in the shade of his dark vision.

They come. His beard has lost its novelty for him; the black is a place to dream. The walk down is faster. No blindfold is needed, for it remains unlit until the last steps, until the candles shatter his senses in an agony of brilliance.

When he raises his sight to the veiled ones, he sees them standing facing him; all nod once and he is dragged away through a side door. He bites his lip, nipping the sounds which squeeze through. His knees sag but the fingers clutch him, his toes skin and lose some nails as they take him down another flight of underground stairs.

It is a wooden table they strap him upon. The lights are of torches and the walls are grey bricks. The blackness crowds in, but torches circle the chamber in a ring of shadows.

The black suits stand on each side of the table; the purple ones file in, their robes swishing the ground, their veils in place. All assemble about him and sway, candles in gloved fists.

"Why?" he asks.

Masks raise and stare across his body into other masks.

"Why?" is the answer.

The mountain in the distance is never reached by the climbers. It sits a day away, snow upon its peak and pines roughing down its slopes to the shaggy forest at its feet before the town where live the mightiest of climbers.

In spring, many encouraged by the youth of the year take up picks and spikes, but these never return. Some may even have conquered the crest. In summer, some vacationers start, but the meadows along the way welcome them to spread their fat lunches. The fall turns the adventurous back to their harvests from which their imaginations have never strayed too far, and winter finds all curled in huts with lusty wives; they thump their mates' bellies in hope of finding themselves.

The circle of forms about him disappears through the dark exit, lighting up the exit with the passing through of their candles, and now the torches burn. Blackness draws in their lowering wicks. The bonds about him chafe his skin; his feet itch from scabs and scalp tingles with sweat.

Through the entrance slides a white form. It hesitates. He strains to stare. "Yes," he says. "Yes, come, come to me."

It comes tipping. A white gown covers its moist lines. Its breasts poke out in tips. The white gown falls to the tops of her toes, sweeping the circle of her stride. Above the angular neck floats her narrow black face. High cheekbones and stub nose are planted beneath the wide arching eyes and short black kinky hair tops all.

"I've waited so long," he says. "Can you?"

She nods; her dark eyes tease but she nods. The wicks sputter.

"Now," he says. "NOW!"

And darkness slides in like a giant gull's shadow to roost with the last torches' breath, and she slinks with cat grace to his feet, and with her darting fiery tongue, licks his soles until he pleads to be saved from . . .

In the Wine Time

S he passed the corner in small ballerina slippers, every evening during my last wine time, wearing a light summer dress with big pockets, swinging her head back and to the side all special-like, hearing a private melody singing in her head. I waited for her each dusk, and for this she granted me a smile, but on some days her selfish tune would drift out to me in a hum; we shared the smile and sad tune and met for a moment each day but one of that long-ago summer.

The times I would be late she lingered, in the sweltering twilight, at the corner in the barber shop doorway, ignoring the leers and coughs from within, until she saw me hurrying along the tenement fronts. On these days her yellows and pinks and whites would flash out from the smoked walls, beckoning me to hurry hurry to see the lights in her eyes before they fleeted away above the single smile, which would turn about and then down the street, hidden by the little pretty head. Afterwards, I would stand before the shop refusing to believe the slander from within.

"Stevie . . . why do you act so stupid?" Liz asked each day I arose to await the rendezvous.

"I don't know . . . just do, that's all," I always explained.

"Well, if you know you're being a fool, why do you

go on moonin' out there in the streets for *that*?"

"She's a friend of mine, Liz . . . she's a friend."

August dragged in the wake of July in steaming sequence of sun and then hell and finally sweltering night. The nights found me awake with Cliff and Liz and our bottles of port, all waiting for the sun to rise again and then to sleep in dozes during the miserable hours. And then for me to wake hustling my liquor money and later to wait on the corner for my friend to pass.

"What'd the hell you say to her, Steve?" Cliff asked.

"Nothin'."

"Nothing?"

"Nawh . . . nothin'."

"Do you ever try?"

"Nawh," I said.

"Why? She's probably just waitin' for you to . . ."

"Nawh she's not. We don't need to say anything to each other. We know all we want to find out."

And we would go on like that until we were so loaded our voices would crack and break as fragile as eggs and the subject would escape us, flapping off over the roofs like a fat pigeon.

Summer and Cliff and Liz and me together—all poured from the same brew, all hating each other and loving, and consuming and never forgiving—but not letting go of the circle until the earth swung again into winter, bringing me closer to manhood and the freedom to do all the things that I had done for the past three summers.

We were the group, the gang. Cliff and Liz entangled within their union, soon to have Baby Dan, and Hester, and Skunky, and Dee Dee, and maybe who knows who by now. Summer and me wrapped in our embrace like lovers, accepting each as an inferior, continually finding faults and my weaknesses, pretending to forgive though never forgetting, always at each other's vitals . . . My coterie and my friend . . . She with the swinging head and flat-footed stance and the single smile and private song for me.

She was missing for a day in the last week of summer.

I waited on the corner until the night boiled up from the pavements and the wine time approached too uncomfortably.

Cliff didn't laugh when he learned of my loss; Liz stole half a glass more than I should have received. The night stewed us as we blocked the stoop fighting for air and more than our shares of the port, while the bandit patrol cruised by as sinister as gods.

She was there waiting the next day, not smiling nor humming but waving me near. I approached and saw my very own smile.

"I love you, little boy," she said.

I nodded, trying to comprehend.

"You're my little boy, aren't you?" She took my hand. "I have to go away but I wanted to tell you this before I left." She looked into my eyes and over my shaggy uncut hair. "I must be years older than you, but you look so much older than I. In two more years you won't be able to stop with only wine," she said. "Do you have to do it?"

"I don't know . . . just do, that's all," I explained.

"I'm sorry, my dear," she said. "I must go now."

"Why?"

"I just must."

"Can I go with you?"

She let go of my hand and smiled for the last time.

"No, not now, but you can come find me when you're ready."

"But where?" I asked.

"Out in the world, little boy, out in the world. Remember, when you're ready, all you have to do is leave this place and come to me; I'll be waiting. All you'll need to do is search!"

Her eyes lighted for the last time before hiding behind the pretty head, swinging then away from me, carrying our sorrowful, secret tune.

I stood listening to the barber shop taunts follow her into the darkness, watching her until the wicked city night captured her; then I turned back to meet autumn and Cliff and Liz in our last wine time, meeting the years which had to hurry hurry so I could begin the search that I have not completed.

The Helper

"You the helper?" she asks, peering through the cracked slit between door and frame. He nods.

"Well, come on in." The door is shut; he hears the chain clatter and the spring of the lock snapping before the hold button's click, and she is pulling the door open as he walks into the narrow hallway.

Her sandy hair is tied by a bandana and the blue Levi's are faded dull.

"My husband ain't here now; he's gone to rent a trailer and car. My daddy and him will be back directly and they can help us."

The dining room is crowded with boxes, filled and tied, and chairs are stacked in corners, around tables and stands, and among piles of movables. It is a three-room apartment; one bedroom, a living room, a dining area and kitchen behind, with the bathroom off the hallway. In the front room, a television chassis sits empty, gaping and hollow, as the tube lies upon the floor, beside the shell, a squat cyclops. At the end of the hallway, opposite the living room doorway, is the bedroom.

"Have a seat, won't you?" she says, leading him into the front room.

Sunshine upon the curtainless panes gleams through the clearness, flashing over the floor, reflecting down the hallway and back to the front, in the bedroom, and outside along the ivied sides of the building to burn over the leaves until reaching farther, the rays trace out the pattern of the kitchen window and scorch through. The curtains are stacked atop a clothes hamper which bulges with top ajar. A calendar of a cowgirl, in only holsters and spurs, her crimson nails clashing with the flash of her silver pistols, takes aim, hanging from the wall above the television. The helper's eyes cross to where the cowgirl's gun barrels point toward the bridge of his nose.

The room he and the girl sit in is done in pink, with white baseboards slicing the pastel blocks of the walls into rectangles, the woodwork leading around corners and up the halls and framing the bedroom and kitchen, to stream flooding in a pool of glare, sun-dashed and stark, striking out like the sun's mirror from the painted white bathroom. Rolled and tied upon the bathroom floor is a scruffy white rug.

"Would you like some coffee?" she asks.

"Yes, black, please."

Chubby hands smooth down the girl's sides, smoothing themselves against the bulges of her sides and pants as she steps into the kitchen.

"You sure you don't want anything in your coffee?" she calls from the kitchen.

He doesn't reply. From his seat on the couch, the man is trapped in the net of morning sunlight. A trickle of sweat starts down his back, but he sits moving his back against the pillows, not allowing his fingers to scratch, pressing the crawling sensation away.

"Here you go," the girl returns with his cup and saucer. "You sure you don't want anything in it?"

"No, thank you."

She goes to the kitchen and returns clicking the cup upon her saucer. She takes a seat across from him and smiles from a hassock. He sips from his cup, the steam and sun keeping his face moist.

"Are you in school?" the girl asks.

"No, not now."

"Oh . . . I thought the Employment Office would send us a college boy."

The helper takes another sip.

"We asked for a college boy who needed some extra work," she says.

Her cup is filled with a creamy mixture and she quaffs it down in gulps, then stands looking at his nearly filled cup.

"We're going back up north," she says. "My husband and me . . . we're going back to college in Oregon."

"That's nice."

She walks past the couch, her floppy workshirt brushing his chin, and peers out the window, looking each way up the one-way street.

"You don't have ta . . ." she begins and steps back to the center of the room as he rises.

"That's okay. I'm a slow coffee drinker and I might as well begin," he says, picking up one of the nearer cardboard boxes.

She scurries to the hall door, her tennis shoes squealing upon the hardwood surface.

"Well, if you want to start now I don't see anything wrong with it," she says, opening the door. "Here, let me show you where to put those things until my husband comes."

Her topknot bobs and springs across the rag tying

her head as she flounces down the stairs leading him to the wide entrance hall. Two wooden chairs sit on each side of a table in the hall. Mirrors line each side of the walls leading to the outside door.

As the helper lowers the box he looks at his reflection in the mirror, watching the trail of sweat trickle to the end of his nose. From beyond his shoulder he sees her eyes in the glass.

"Well, I'll open this outside door and get things ready for my dad and husband when they come," she says when he turns.

Upstairs, the items wait. The boxes lining the walls of the room, the pieces wrapped or tied or turned upon their sides. In a corner, beside a basket of newspaper-wrapped dishes, lies an upturned campaign sign, stick pointed at the ceiling, the upside-down candidate smiling lipless out of a dark blue background. The helper bends for another box and turns toward the hall doorway for his trip below, leaving the poster grinning at his back.

"Ah . . . here's our little helper," a stout woman says when he reaches the bottom of the stairs. The woman is wearing a crimson silk Chinese coolie outfit; large brass bracelets swing from her wrists, smaller loops pull her earlobes low; tied about one puffed ankle is a golden chain with a knotted heart, and grass thongs upon her feet make shuffling sounds.

"This is my mother," the girl says.

"Here, young man," the woman points, "you can put that box down here." She steps out of the helper's path. "That's darling of you," she says to his bending rear.

"My husband and dad are out front hitching up the trailer," the girl says.

The helper starts up the stairs for another load.

"Sister, it looks like you've got a good start," the woman tells the girl.

Upstairs, the helper sees many of the boxes gone, moved by his successive trips; only several piles of the smaller items remain to be moved; the last to go are the large and vital goods.

"YOO HOO UP THERE!" the woman downstairs yells. "SOMEONE WILL BE UP TO GIVE YOU A HAND WITH THE REST OF THOSE THINGS!"

As he finishes his morning coffee, heavy steps bound up the stairs. A gangling man with glasses tilting on the edge of his nose enters, wearing white coveralls with the insignia of an international airline.

"You've really got this place cleaned out," the tall man says, looking through the room. "Well, we might as well get the table tennis equipment this trip." He lifts one end of the green table.

"Ohhh . . . be careful, fellows," the woman says as the edge of the broad table is twisted around the last stairwell. "Be careful, Buddy." She addresses the tall man. "You remember the awful jar that boy gave the piano last summer in Hawaii?"

"Yes, I remember, Mother," the man says.

She smiles at the helper and pats him on the shoulder when he crosses the last step; her jewelry gives her a jangle.

"Oh, you both must be so tired to bring that thing down," she says. "Your sweating brings out such gorgeous tones in your skin." She peers at the helper's face. "I had this houseboy in Kingston . . ." The woman talks as the two men tramp through the hall. "Buddy," she calls as they reach the door, sweeping the swishing sleeves of her suit in a swirl toward the street, "take it right out to the trailer."

"Yes, that's where we're going," the man says.

The girl and a middle-aged man are loading the last of the boxes into the largest trailer made for autos. The trailer is painted orange and twin doors in the rear are fastened back along the sides. Chairs and hassocks and picture frames crowd the loading zone. The trailer is hitched to a new Dodge.

"Here, Buddy, bring that table here," the middle-aged man says. His neck is freckled red and brown and his paunch is solid. He is dressed in grey industrial trousers, green plaid woodsman shirt, and brown crepe-soled shoes. He squints incessantly and there are the indentations of glasses straddling his nose.

The tall man and the helper swing the large table around in back of the trailer; the table legs are folded in and under; the net and paddles have been stowed in some box.

"Slide it along the side, Buddy," the girl says. "Daddy, don't you think he should put it up against the side?"

"Yeah, slide it up that side next to them boxes, Buddy." The man points out the slot where the table tennis table is to go.

"Oh, the little precious babies . . . don't you dare frighten them," the mother says upstairs, to Buddy and the helper when they reach to take the fish tank.

Sliding along the top of the glass, the water reaches the edge and spills a puddle over the side before they balance the container.

"Ohhh, dear, oh Buddy, please be careful with the

poor darlings," the mother says. "Remember, I got that aquarium in Hong Kong."

"Damn, where are we going to put that thing?" the old man says, as he sees little room in the trailer.

"We can't leave them, Dad," the girl says.

A grey sky breeze splashes the surface of the water and the girl's hair blows over her eyes. Through a cloud-slit, the sun heats the fronts of buildings on the far side of the street, but the wind fusses with the skirts of the awnings, as if they were petticoats.

"Here"—the father leads them to the car in front—"put it on the seat." They grope with the glass container until it rests firmly upon the cushions; they wedge boxes and bags against its sides.

The three men walk back to the trailer and look in; it seems as though nothing else can fit.

"Go on up and get the rest," the old man says. "Sister and me will move some of these things around."

"Now, take special care with Augustus's cage," the mother warns the helper as he lifts the parrot's cage. A black leather cover shrouds the large square prison, but the bird flutters within the dark. "Don't let him see your fingers or he'll bite; I warn you."

With caution, the helper traces his way downstairs to the outside. Buddy follows with the dart board and darts, and he carries one of the bowling balls in its special fabric carrier.

"But, we can't get any more in," the girl says.

"Just a minute now," the father says, pulling at the center of the mass.

"Let me help you, Dad." The tall man assists.

"Herbert, if you shove that crate I got in Delhi down

to . . ." The mother shoves her way to the front.

Ten minutes later the helper comes out the door holding a rubber plant. "You're going along marvelously, fellows," the mother says.

"Gee, I never knew we had so much," the girl says. "We're the Beverly Hillbillies . . . Jesus, we're the Beverly Hillbillies," she mutters several times.

After the center is cleared once more, the chairs are stacked in the very front instead of the sides and rear. The side opposite the table tennis table is left empty for the bed.

The sun is gone and chill waits in the shade. The breeze flutters the loose spreads and papers in the boxes and corners of the project, and a yellow painted Volkswagen parks at one of the buildings across the street. In its window is a sign in red. SCABS MUST GO! A leather-jacketed man gets out and enters the building.

"Weee . . . that wind's almost as bad as the one we got last time in Fairbanks," the woman says to her husband, daughter and son-in-law.

"Now, after these card tables, I want you to get the rest of the potted plants, and then the encyclopedias and golf bags," the girl says as Buddy and the helper clear the last of the items from the apartment. "Then there's only the mattress and the bed springs left, and the T.V. and chassis . . . and don't forget the bathroom rug, the clothes in the closets and my bowling ball."

The father comes into the room and looks about the empty walls; he stoops and lifts the upturned campaign poster, wedging it under his arm, making his arm a banner and blindfold across the eyes of the candidate. Written at the bottom of the still wrong-way picture are the words: IN YOUR HEART YOU KNOW HE'S RIGHT!

The helper is busy finding a grip on the chassis.

"There won't be room for the chassis," the old man says to the tall one.

"Oh, it don't matter anyway, Dad," Buddy says. "I got the set and can put it in any old chassis."

"Well, leave it down in the hall and me and Ma will come back this evening and take it over to our place."

With a turn of his neck, the older man looks about the room once more, then walks to the cowgirl calendar and eases it off its nail and places it under his arm, opposite the politician. Bowlegged, he goose-steps from the room, the ends of the pictures flapping behind the seat of his pants, showing secrets of themselves: cowgirl buttocks, campaigner, silvery gun, IN YOUR HEART, rump, smile, gun, IN YOUR HEART, ass, leer, murder, IN YOUR HEART . . .

"You boys sure did a good job," the mother says when they wrestle the box spring to the trailer, discarding the frame and soiled mattress, promising to get better ones up north.

Upstairs, the helper looks through the rooms and closets for anything forgotten; he finds the girl in the bedroom changing her pants.

"Is there anything else, Miss?" he asks.

"WILL YOU PLEASE PARDON ME!"

He walks downstairs and approaches the trailer. The gangly man opens his wallet and pulls out several bills and hands them to the helper.

"Thanks," he says.

The tall man nods.

Before the helper turns to leave he catches the father's stare for the first time: "See you again, boy," the old man smiles and salutes with a sloppy wave.

The helper smiles, nods, pocketing his money, and turns down the street.

In New England Winter

We picked Chuck up at noon and drove with brood hanging close to our bodies blended with the sweat. The '53 burped reliably in its infirmity; its windows gulped the grit which peppered my face, and Indian summer rode with us across the city, a spent brave, a savage to the last, causing me visions of winter in New England . . .

In New England winter we played gin rummy and groped nudely under the patched quilt. While we each read the other's thoughts erroneously, I chanted Whitman as she curled in a corner with Superman and Mickey Spillane. We shrilled from the moment's gratification under the quilt; it was our bond of permanence in the cold times.

"Steve?"

"Yeah, Art," I said.

"Feel okay?"

"Sure."

"How 'bout you, Chuck?" Art asked.

"Great, man."

The car turned off Spring and then in and about some side streets before heading again south on Broad. Chuck was a hell of a driver; I was glad he was at the wheel even though I don't dig him. Just maybe, just maybe with Chuck, I might get back to winter and New England . . .

We danced to something called bebop around the potbellied stove in my single set of pajamas, ate like gluttons from her lone pot, and drank a daily jug of muscatel from our mayonnaise jar. The jar was cherished; the common spittle was as personal as we dared be. We loathed to bathe to wash the other's funk away; each ate his fish-ends and black-eyed peas and drank when he could, but all nourishment was a trifle compared to our daily fare, for we fed with gusto upon the other's store of dream . . .

"Well . . . this is the place, Steve," Art said.

"We're here," Chuck filled in.

"Yeah . . . I know," I said.

"Sure she'll kick over?" Art asked Chuck.

"If it don't, we's got a long run."

Art and I got out on the street side, adjusting our sunglasses and stretching confidently. We walked around the corner and climbed narrow stairs to the second floor. There were only two people in the finance co's office; the rest were at lunch like I had planned. I walked to the counter; Art, certain, trailed my heels.

The blonde had been in my freshman class in high school. Our distance had prevented her from ever knowing me, but I did catch her once staring around me, staring as I stare at the silhouette of my shadow.

"Good afternoon, sir." She smiled as she had learned, fastening her stare upon my glasses' frame. "May I help you?"

"Yes, you may." She seemed so fragile standing in my gun's way, awaiting its punishment. "Don't say anything . . . just don't give me any trouble and don't say a word."

We tied them; I twisted the ropes about the blonde's wrists so she would never forget. Art gathered the money easily and locked it in his briefcase; it was all finished in seven minutes. The best job was over and done; it was finished and I was done, all over and done . . .

Ice grows upon windowpanes in New England winter. The dread of it entering our world caused her nightmares; but, I didn't dare claim these, so I awoke her and soothed her chatters with the jar. And afterwards, we promised ourselves that somehow we would find a stop for haunting yesterdays and tomorrows which waited to be refused. Our futures loomed bitter and less bearable than the snowdrifts blocking the alleys below; but our fears seared, raging about our souls, fanning a combustion of brutality. As my manhood leaked away upon the wintry streets by day, she cemented together my backbone under the patched quilt through the long long icy nights . . .

There were thirteen hundred four dollars and thirty-two cents for my share after we counted the money at Art's place.

"You're a genius, Steve," Art raved, congratulating himself for teaming with me.

"He sure is," Chuck said.

"Well you guys know what to do . . . just don't flash your rolls . . . and keep your goddamn mouths shut!"

"Sure, Steve."

"Yeah, man . . . you knows we ain't no punks."

I patted my wallet, making its bulge less awkward, and adjusted my glasses.

"I'll see you guys," I said.

"Okay, Steve," Art said, "call when you want me."

"Forget it . . . I won't be calling . . . ever."

"What d'ya mean?" Chuck asked.

"I'm through . . . that's what I mean . . . don't ever expect to see me again . . . and if you do bump into me, just act like ya never knew me."

Art usually knew how to take me. "Well . . . then take care, Professor." He offered his hand; I gripped it harder than I should, but it might be the last time I ever saw my brother.

"Thanks, Art," I said.

"Got any plans?" Chuck said.

"Yeah . . . a couple . . . a couple of very simple ones," I said as I stepped out of the door and shut it tightly.

Yeah, two very simple ones, I thought, as I stepped out into dying autumn.

Two very simple ones: pray for winter and head north.

The Reluctant Voyage

It was a chill day that I chose to return to the waterfront. My last visit had been long before in my childhood, and now in the prime of life, filled with those romantic impressions carried more than a score of years, I anticipated a day's adventure incomparable to my now solitary experiences.

I recognized the cobbled street which ran parallel to the piers by its single track for freight-car unloadings. The street appeared as dingy as ever, but the worn tracks which had before glistened silvery in the sun, were now scarred and crusted with rust, their grooves no longer caught the knives of train wheels but were packed by filth.

Now there were trucks of all sizes passing over the street, but no horsedrawn wagons were evident as they had been a few years ago. And flaring up, a nostalgic spark relit neglected memories, as I turned a corner after walking hours, and found the ferry-depot boarded up. The ferry, which ran no longer, had taken my loved ones and me on excursions along the coast, and on special trips, to barren sandbars lying off the point. I tried to gather the past images and meld them, to piece them into some beloved whole, but the great red and white sign of the boat station distracted me. It hung askew, slapping the side of the long, covered wharf, above the grey waves which approached the structure like hunters, dark and shadowy, stalking their prey until, too near to restrain themselves, they rose up and heaved frothy white with a rush and dashed terribly about the building's supports, trying vainly to pull it from its foundation, to swarm over it, drowning and stomping it.

Even the gulls had deserted this area and remained at nest today. The cold was severe, but I knew that gulls do not easily surrender to nature. I had once seen one of these strong flyers farther north, in a place where fresh water comes to meet the sea; the poor creature had assumed that all water is the same. In the cold of the day, it had lazed like a duck upon the serene surface of a lake until the water had frozen, trapping the white soarer in the ice. I watched the bird from ashore and felt pangs of conscience with each scream from it, for I was unable to aid it; the ice was not strong enough to support my weight. I watched the bird beating its helpless body with its single wing which had not frozen into the lake also; it stretched its white neck to the heavens, attempting with all its energies to break from the hardened water, but the skies waited without caring, not welcoming the creature to release itself into the vastness of freedom as the bird had previously done. And even its excited squawks finally seemed to fly back into the captive's throat, for the winds arose and blustered across the icy landscape, sweeping all petty things back and away. I abandoned the creature to the lake and had not thought of it until now, probably because a gull-less waterfront is quite unnatural.

"Get out of the doorway, you there!" a voice boomed behind my back. I started as I would have done as a youth and became angered that someone would use a tone of voice to me in that manner. I spun around.

He stood tall and dour. His pea jacket seemed to be a casing enclosing a steely rod. As I turned upon him, he only stared past me to the boarded doorway.

"Is that any way to speak to a man, sir?" I asked.

"I have my ship to meet, young man; please get out of my way."

I looked into his face which was clean-shaven but shadowy grey from a perpetual beard. His eyes were as grey as his chin and frosty drifts of white brows piled at the bottom of his forehead in an unbroken snowy turf.

"I'm sorry to have delayed you, sir," I said. "Are you sure this is the correct wharf? This place doesn't appear to have been used for years."

He didn't reply but brushed me rudely aside, pulling what appeared to me a small dogcart, the type I had seen during my last voyages through the eastern islands. The gaunt figure took the rusted handle in his long hand and pulled the great double doors apart as easily as I draw open my cupboard. The tearing of weathered nails and the splintering of lumber might have been only a squeaky hinge to the pea-coated man. After he had thrown the doors apart, he entered through and called to me over his shoulder.

"What are you waiting for, mate? We haven't forever!"

I followed him, my hopes for adventure seemingly realized. We walked through the long shed to the opposite doorway which was the exit to the boat landing. The tall stranger pulled these doors open as simply as the first. The clouded daylight startled me, though the walk through the black building had only taken a few moments. The man was pointing out to sea as my eyes adjusted to the glare.

"Look," he said. "For that, I came so far."

Upon the horizon was a speck with a puff of black smoke trailing it.

"They're burning too rich a mixture in their fires," I said.

"Yes, mate," he said. "They are eager to see their captain."

I looked about the pier, watching the waves lunging up to grab the rotting wood. In some places the pursuers had clutched sections and dragged them down; I saw the face of the sea through the holes, as the currents stalked back and forth as hungered as sharks, and I shuddered to think of being in their jaws.

"The ship is here," the captain shouted to me above the harsh call of the waves. I knew he was mistaken, for the ship had not time to cross the distance. But it was there when I looked again back in its direction, tied up with gangplank lowered.

"Quickly, mate," the captain said and rushed forward, pulling his cart, inviting disaster, unmindful of the many traps gaping through the dock. I sped after him, running with all of my strength, but he easily beat me to the gangplank, even pulling lengths ahead of me, though I am a hearty sprinter, as I put on a killing burst of speed toward the last. He awaited me; and when I came up to him he put his hand against my chest and pushed me back.

"Hold up a moment, man," he said. "There's someone coming over the side."

I blew like a horse with steam flying from my nostrils and with body heaving. I wanted to tell him I was not coming aboard, but I had no breath to expel the message.

From down the gangplank raced a young man of my age, dressed in whites. He saluted aft and then to the captain, in two quick motions, and extended his hand to me saying, "Good voyage, mate."

"But, I'm not going aboard," I said to the man in whites. "And why are you wearing your summer uniform in such vicious weather?"

"It's as it has to be," he said. "Don't worry, I'll remain here at the pier and stand by." He hefted a life preserver and played out its long rope and made several vigorous movements, testing the line's elasticity.

The tall man, whom I had ignored, took my hand and dragged me up the gangplank. I struggled with him, for I can be a wolf when enraged, but I was a helpless being in his grip. He pulled me and the cart along together. Then the gangplank sped up after us, almost knocking me aside, before the captain had completely towed me upon deck.

"I don't want to come aboard," I shouted at him. He unloosed his grasp upon me and bounded to the pilothouse. The ship was already under way, drawing swiftly from land. The young sailor, left behind, ran back and forth upon the pier waving, hailing, indicating the line still in his hands.

"I don't want to go with you," I screamed toward the bridge. "Turn back!"

The land had now almost descended into the obscurity of twilight and distance. I sprang to the rail and threw off my jacket and shoes. I knew that I must leap from the side, cutting the water cleanly and deep, far under and away from the ripping ship's screws.

I held my breath and braced, waiting for the ship to keel toward leeward so that I could dive safely ahead of the waves which would soon pound against the hull. But before I leaped, I looked into the cold, grey face of the sea bulging like a grim, billowing curtain which waited to surely shade me forever, and then I knew that I would never leave this ship until its master willed. And before I sank back to the deck, to lie wallowing aghast against the gunnels, welcoming the waves to break coldly over me but unable to snatch me away, I looked toward the bridge where my captain stood. He was staring with vacant, grey eyes seaward toward the bitter horizon.

Travel from Home

August showers scalded our streets during the days, and the nights were without sleep from the steam and sweat. Groups of black figures crouched on each doorstoop, muttering among themselves, their eyes lit by the insect-fanned streetlights, but some pulled down long draughts from half-hidden bottles and wine jugs, and others embraced and groped, waiting for the hour before dawn when they could return to bed.

"C'mon, make dat point, mother!" Little Willy moaned.

"Can't beat you and yo prayers too, little nigger," Big Willy growled.

"Sev-vannn . . . mama . . . sev-vannn . . . haaahhh . . ."

Little Willy made his point.

The summer night crap game under the streetlamp was ending; the money was as tight as our tensions.

Some of us don't play, just stand on the corner under the light, ready to signal our boys when the cops cruise up, before their blue and grey pig eyes saw what they knew would be there, and before they leaped from the patrol car, scattering us into the shadows, and then picking up the coins left in the lighted circle of emptiness. And some of us only waited for the moment.

It was about three when he passed across the street in front of the billboard, head held stiffly, feet padding along like a penguin's. Eyes watched the pale stranger cross the billboard front, step into Cadence Street, no bigger than most alleys, and waddle up on the curb on the far side and pass the hollow windows of the vacant butcher shop.

"Da ho'ays, must'ta turned dat trick out early," Red said, watching him, noticing his hurried movements. He saw me check out the stranger. "Let's take him, Chuck," he said, then waiting for my move, sprang off at a lope.

I jogged behind, hearing Little Willy holler, "C'mon, mother," and tested the looseness of my legs.

He heard us and tore out in a dash. And we were after him. Red and I started pumping hard but still allowed him to keep his lead, waiting for his flabby legs to give. At the corner he turned, stretching out for the long straightaway up 13th Street hill.

When we hit the corner he was a third up the block, and the incline of the night street was clear before us except for the galloping figure, and I knew the race was mine.

"Turn it on, Chuck," I heard Red yell as I passed, my shirt waving behind, the blackness of night and revenge in my conked red mop.

Eyes on the doorstoops followed us, bearing down with me on the victim in that good race. The air in its summer heaviness pushed, the moist tone and taste of night in city without trees or grass was what mingled with the funk of sweat and terror. The air weighted my lungs and held back his thick body. Our distance tightened like the raw lips of a wound; the far corner was a third of a block away, but I knew that I would see his blood before he reached the intersection.

He staggered, jerking his legs in a frantic effort to find control, and then he sprawled beside a trash can, his arms coming up, using the can of filth for support. I smashed my fist aside his head before he came off his knees; he rolled with some cans as they spilled across the curb; he wailed, kicking out at shadows. Red came puffing up and planted one of his long "old folks' comforts" in a kidney.

"OH LORD . . ." the stranger screamed. "OH LORD JESUS!"

"HEY, WHAT YOU BOYS DOIN'?" Some older people ran from their stoops. "WHAT YOU DOIN' TO DAT WHITE MAN?" a mammy-lookin' woman said.

As the white man spun away from the soggy thumps of Red's shoes, I waited for his dribbling mouth with a chopping left hook and a straight right which split a knuckle.

"Oh Lord, Oh Lord," he whimpered on his back. "Lord God . . . have mercy on me."

We all call on him at least once.

"ACCEPT THE SAVIOUR, THE LORD JESUS," the white missionary lady said in the skid row rescue. The room: half-filled for the evening meal of beans and bread with coffee having a detergent tang. But we homeless and drunken had to first wait on the Lord.

"Kiss mah ass," one friend said to another, his arm about the man's bloodied head.

"What . . . ?" the bloodied man replied. "Shussck maah dick!"

"HE WILL FORGIVE YOU YOUR SINS . . . HE WILL . . ." the preacher lady continued.

"Wha don ya come home with me, ah could hold ya in mah arms all night," the pushy one said.

"Get ya hands offa me, ya creep."

"C'mon, it ain't no sex involved . . . sex is da fardest thing from my mind . . ." He tried to cradle the other man's bleeding head.

"JESUS . . . JESUS . . . JESUS IS . . ." the preacher lady began singing.

". . . it's just dat you's human," the drunk said.

"Shussck mah dick!" His friend pulled away.

"GODDAMMIT!" a woman screamed and hovered about them. Her short height tied her obvious muscles into a ball of biceps. "YOU BASTARDS," she said rolling up her sleeves, flexing her arms and shaking a red fist in their faces.

"Shut up! Can't decent worshippers of the Lord get some respect? . . . RESPECT!!! . . . what you're gettin', you no good bastards!"

"Jesus . . . Jesus . . . Jesus . . ." the preacher lady crooned.

The two drunks frowned at each other and mumbled to themselves.

"JESUS . . . JESUS . . . JESUS . . ." the preacher lady raised her voice on the last chorus.

"*Respect* . . ." the muscled woman whispered the threat for the last time and sulked back to her seat.

"*Shussck our dicks*," one of the drunks whispered, and they sat holding each other and mumbling, waiting for their beans and bread and cleansing coffee.

"He's a fag!" I heard Red tell the woman and two men as I dragged the maimed man out of the street and propped him aside a pole. The group of snoopers were drunk, or they wouldn't have interfered.

"You mean he's a queer?" one of the men asked.

"Yeah," Red said.

Sniggers rustled in the night.

"Jesus . . . I wish you'd kill the paddy mathafuk-ker," the big woman said and turned to move away with blackness surrounding her.

One of the men followed. Soon only one shadow stood by. Seeing the remaining man, the stranger tried to twist out of my hands.

"Please . . ." he started, arms outstretched, and I sagged him with a gut punch. He vomited on my shoes.

"Mathafukker!" I kicked him in the face, feeling his teeth give.

"Don't hurt him real bad, boys," the man said from the darkness.

"We ain't . . . just showin' him a lesson, that's all," Red said.

"Damn, you guys really work over a sonna bitch, don't ya," the drunken voice said.

"We ain't gonna hurt him anymo'," Red said. "Just talk ta him and find out why he's messin' 'round here fo."

Then there was no one under the light but Red and me and him; he began to cry.

The poor lonely bastard.

"HEY, BOY," the bleary-eyed old man said. "Hey, boy, help me, will ya? Thank ya, son, will ya wheel me in here so I can get somethin' ta eat?

"Here's a table . . . get me a bowl of soup, will ya, and you get anything you want . . .

"Only coffee! Hey, get yourself anything you want. Get it, I say, ya want me ta slap ya?

"Ya just got ta town? From where? . . . Oh! Been in jail! I just got out myself, ya know, kept gettin' drunk. When I got out, the only guy would help me was a colored boy, yeah, pushed me all over town . . . that boy was really okay; I bet I took him in over a dozen restaurants and the only thing he ever got was nit nats. Yeah, just like you . . . nit nats.

"Here's the change . . . here, take it. HERE TAKE IT, YA . . . ! Ohhh . . . take it, fellah . . . I want ya ta have it.

"He never would eat a full meal . . . only one who helped me . . . Hey, boy, where ya goin'! . . . Come back here when I tell ya . . . COME BACK!"

I smashed him once more in the face; his head bounced on the pavement.

"Cool it, Chuckie," Red said to me.

I turned away, breathing deep; I could feel the many eyes back in the darkness; eyes cursing us; eyes hating us for doing the things the eyes wished to see.

Red handed me some bills in a wad; the blood from my busted hands wet them before I shoved the money into my pocket.

"Everything's straight, baby?" Red asked. I looked at him. He gave me the hit's ring; he kept the watch.

The game was over when we got back to the corner; it took close to an hour to describe the chase and the mugging.

"Yeah, I told some people he was queer and they just went 'bout dere business," Red repeated over and over.

"Hey, Chuck, tell us what happened on the road before you got busted and came back," Little Willy said.

"Yeah, you always makin' it somewheres, man. You's worse den some fukkin' hobo!"

"Where you go every summer, Chuckie?" Big Willy had asked too, before the cruiser had crept up, and the cop had shouted out the window that somebody had just stomped a fag on 13th Street, and that he wanted our corner and we better get our "black asses out of sight, pronto!"

"Wow, man, if he had'a searched us we'd been fucked," Red had said before we split.

"Yeah, he never thought we'd be lame enough to stand around bull shittin' 'bout it."

That morning as Red and I walked to our block through the early, deserted streets, me holding my aching fists, with the dawn glowing about us, Red said: "Yeah, Chuck . . . where do you go every year?"

"Man . . . it ain't far enough . . . it just ain't."

Mister Newcomer

She was the single person ahead of me. The door stood locked, and we waited. Her girdle and halter tied her swells down but not completely. She wore open-back heels; I knew she was a Southerner.

"I guess we'll get seats," I said.

"Ah huhh, I guess we will."

I learned her name, that she had been born in Mississippi, where she worked and how much she made in less than the ten minutes before the door was opened by the short instructor. I knew I would make the girl in less than a week. I told her my birthplace, name, and lied about my address and past.

"I was between jobs and had a little cash, so here I am, Catherine."

Catherine rested her arm next to mine in class. The class excited me. The instructor was hardly older than me and bragged from the first of doing his final work toward his Ph.D. He talked in a special vocabulary that none of that class of daytime clerks and shop girls knew, but I had picked up on some of it from having read a little literary history. I shot him a few questions that seemed to please him and in answering he soared above all our heads with his newly acquired university knowledge.

I had been away from a real school for years, and

if this was a school and learning then this was where I belonged. There are too many books I hadn't read . . . There were too many words I needed to know. (What is the origin of turnpike?)

Who was Aristotle and what's his noise? I had to learn quickly and well.

"He likes you," she said as we walked toward her bus stop.

"We do seem to get along."

"Don't be so modest. He likes you because you're one of his best students."

"It's too soon to say that. Just because I've read a few books—"

"Maybe not but it helps. You've got it made in that class; you've got 'college bound' written all over you."

"It shows, huh?"

"Sho . . . what made you stay out of school so long?"

"It has been long, I guess. At least for high school. I quit in the first half of the tenth grade and bummed around for several years until I got old enough to join the Navy." I told her only half as many lies while waiting for her bus.

"Is that all the education you have?"

"No, I used up my GI Bill in a jerk business school and spent a little while in a private high school before coming out here and enrolling in this adult program."

"You really have a past," she said.

Next Thursday night Kate and I were again in class. We went out for coffee at the break; I hardly noticed her drawl.

That night when we walked to the bus she gave me her address and telephone number. It was certain that I would be over before next week's class meeting.

I felt it was good to know a need could be fulfilled by reaching out and making your wishes known. It was good to have a sharp quick mind and a young hard body; that's all it took.

I had gotten a job with the county a week after I hit town. It was in an old office at the General Hospital typing files and records from midnight till the morning. I had to work the weekends and they gave me Wednesdays and Thursdays off.

Most people had told me that a newcomer couldn't get a job with the county. But I did. My supervisor had wanted a man badly for that shift and wasn't particular where he came from.

And I almost refused to learn to type; it was a requirement to get out of business school, and I only took that business course because I wanted something that was easy to waste my GI Bill on. Besides, some guy had told me the school had five girls to every fellow enrolled.

But I had a knack for typing and the rest of the boring subjects were easy, except English. English was a bitch.

I've always been a nut for reading, but I hate grammar—nouns, verbs, agreement—ugh—it all grabs me the wrong way. I had to take a year of business English and there wasn't one book to read in the damned course but our practice workbooks. But knowing hardly anything about the subject, I was still years ahead of my classmates. The little shabby teacher always put me in the spotlight and the other guys hated my guts within two weeks (I'm glad the chicks didn't).

Getting good grades in English almost became an obsession till I passed the state achievement tests in the upper ten. By then, the education bug had bitten me. I even made the honor roll in that jerk school.

They cheated me of twenty-seven months of education. I took all they had to offer in nine months and after that I shot my big mouth off and fought the teachers. But none of them had any academic background; they were just jerks and have-nots who could be bought cheap and appear to the country cousins and unlearned folks, like myself, as scholars.

A shyster named Blackwell was the president. A bigger phoney I never met. Each semester and during the summer he sent down South all types of literature about his "institution." Harvard could be spoken of in the terms that Blackwell used to seduce high school graduates as far away as Florida, and he did make ludicrous statements like: "You future leaders from Blackwell Institute will someday stand beside alumni from Harvard, Yale, Princeton, etc. . . ." I almost puked each assembly when he made his promises to his charges.

He conned me but also taught what a real education meant and how much I needed one.

I left against Blackwell's advice, before my course was completed in another twenty-seven months, and enrolled in a university-run high school for drop-outs, wayward girls and other misfits, like me, who could afford tuition and pass the entrance exams. It was enriching, if hard work enriches, and I got canned within the year.

Kate's house was fifth in the block. The street was dark and deserted at seven and I bumbled around for twenty minutes before I had nerve enough to walk from lawn to lawn checking the house numbers until I found hers.

I rang once.

"Hello, sweetcake. Come on in out of the night air," she said.

"I thought I told you my name."

"All right, then, *for you.*"

I really go for people addressing me formally. That's one of the things that got me snowed at Blackwell's.

All the students were required to call each other by their surnames. Blackwell said it was good practice for business. After its uniqueness had worn away, I thought it weird.

Calling teen-aged broads Miss So and So got under my skin. I never did learn all of their first names. I slept with several on successive weekends and habitually addressed them in a dignified business manner.

It really gave me gooseflesh when one would groan, "You're so good, Mister, I'm in love with your body." It made me feel as if I came in the sanitized package with the Kotex or condoms.

"Call me by my name, honey, or not at all," I would threaten, but it did little good for I would find myself saying repeatedly, "If it isn't on by Monday, Miss So and So, I'll get something to really fix you up."

And if we hadn't gotten it on, I wonder if I would have called our little bastard Mister or Miss. I've imagined its mother mentioning me to Baby Bastard as ". . . You're just like that goddamned Mr. Mother Fucker of yours."

"You're so cold sometimes," Kate said.

"You just think that; come a little closer."

She pulled beer from the refrigerator and we watched television with my arm about her.

"It's two more damned weeks to payday," I said before I left.

"You get paid only once a month, don't you?"

"Yeah, and it seems like a year."

"This will be your first payday, won't it?"

"Yeah . . . yeah, it will."

"Oh, I'm so selfish. I shouldn't have let you spend the carfare to come all the way over here," she said.

"Damn . . . when I can't afford to catch a bus—"

"But you couldn't afford it," she said. "Now, could you?"

". . . ?"

"Let me give it back to you."

"Are you out of your head?"

I tried to stand.

"Oh, come on now," she said, pushing me back. I felt her tight breasts. "Let me be a friend; I understand how it is when you just get in town."

"Nawh, I'd feel cheap."

"No, you won't. Not when you need it. Wait until I get my purse."

She went into her bedroom and I heard a drawer opening.

"Here take this, it'll last you until payday." She slipped a bill into my shirt pocket.

Waiting under the streetlight at the bus stop, I searched. It was a twenty.

I cashed my paycheck the next day. I hadn't mentioned to Kate that I had been working for a month and had my salary split in bimonthly payments.

I had enough to pick up a seventy-five-buck Buick, pay my room rent for a month and get two five-buck meal tickets. I hadn't spent Kate's gift, but I did over the weekend on a girl in tight pants on Adams.

Kate wasn't waiting the next Tuesday when I walked into class. I looked around at the other students but most ducked their heads or gave saccharine smiles.

It was an American literature class and the stuttering instructor began reading critiques on Steinbeck. My mind wandered, recalling the many different volumes I had enjoyed of his. I remembered many nights at sea, on watch or in my bunk, reading the Monterey series.

And then I heard: "Steinbeck shouldn't be tolerated for his worthless, hopeless characters . . . he shouldn't be tolerated for creating plots to exploit tiring social idealism . . . he shouldn't be tolerated for his . . ."

And somehow my voice was rising above the instructor's: "I don't think we should tolerate the critic."

A hush fell, and the instructor stood above me, stuttering more, sputtering out flecks of sputum. "I thought you came here to get my views as well as those of the author's, sir. I can only give you what I know and believe."

The bell rang. I don't remember walking from the room.

I didn't return the second hour. Before leaving school, I stopped at the desk and got a tuition refund. I arrived at Kate's in fifteen minutes. The porch light was on.

"Hi there, handsome," she greeted and unloosed the screen.

"Hello."

"What's wrong? I couldn't reach you and tell you

that I wouldn't be in school tonight. The guy on the desk at the hotel said he'd never heard of you."

"He's new," I said. "I don't hang around there very much, anyway."

"I'm sorry . . ."

"For what?"

"Oh . . . thanks," she said.

"I wondered where you were and if anything was the matter."

"I bet you did."

"Yeah . . . really. Forget my mood; I get like this sometimes. Now what's wrong?"

"Oh, nothin'." She giggled. "Not really, honey."

"Good, I thought all sorts of things when I didn't see you. That's why I left after the first hour and came over."

"You sure can be sweet when you want to." She moved closer.

"You give me more credit than I'm worth. Wait till you know me better."

"I know you now, honey."

"Maybe you do," I said.

"Do you know what, sweetie?"

"No."

"I'm going to move . . ." she said.

"You are?"

"Yeah, I'm making enough now; I just got a raise. Isn't that great?"

"Yeah . . . I can see your point," I said.

"So, this year I'm not going to go to school; I'm going to make some changes in my life. Find a new place, buy some nice clothes, and settle down and take care of business."

"Sounds good to me," I said.

"Then you think I'm doing the right thing?"

"Sure you are."

She found a bottle of VO in the kitchen and some ginger ale.

"Let's celebrate," she said.

At 11:15 I apologized for having to go to work; I promised to stop by the next evening. She patted and asked if I could be late or be "suddenly" taken ill just this once?

"But I haven't been on the job long enough," I explained.

I kissed her in the doorway, then turned the corner and walked to my car and drove within the speed limit.

I was certain I could never see Catherine again.

Support Your Local Police

S UPPORT YOUR LOCAL POLICE!!! the bumper sticker read. And I should have known better. From the way he slowed in front of me before he got to the toll gate, and from his hesitation and his annoyed, "Ahhh, the hell with it," gesture that he gave me crouched over from the cold. But I should have known not to relax as I ran up behind the car after it stopped, my eyes on that bumper sticker. SUPPORT YOUR LOCAL POLICE!!!

But then the Harrisburg exit of the Pennsylvania Turnpike seemed a gateway to the below-freezing winds, and I had been trying to get any kind of lift for all of two hours.

"Thanks," I said when I got into the car.

"Where you comin' from?"

"New York."

"Been waitin' long?"

"About two hours."

"It's a lousy spot. Where you goin'?" the driver asked.

"San Francisco."

"Boy! You really got a trip ahead of you, haven't you?"

"Yeah, I guess I have."

"Well, I'm only going a few exits down and then I'm going south."

That's how I ended up in Lexington, Virginia. Route 60 goes right through there, and that's where my driver was going, to Lexington.

"The radio says there's a snowstorm comin' from the Midwest."

"Yeah, that's what I heard this morning."

After that it didn't take much prodding from him to get me to take the swing below the Mason Dixon and out of the path of winter. I entered the South almost without looking back.

I told him that I was going to San Francisco to get married, and find a good job. He seemed to believe that my fiancee's name was Patsy Mae and that she worked in a laundry, pressing shirts, and that I usually found work as a janitor or in a car wash.

That's the story I usually use when hitchhiking all over the country, to everyone. Marriage, and janitor or car wash. I've learned that that story works on nearly all of them. For hours I can spin out fantasy about my Patsy Mae and how good life is going to be for us, especially if I get work in a good firm out west, like Dow or Lockheed or Boeing. And how California is famous with us colored people all across the country for them wonderful lifetime jobs. I tell these stories with a straight face and some-times talk so much about Patsy Mae that the more brainy of my benefactors become bored with my conversation.

But I know better than to tell them that I am a writer, especially a playwright, and that I'm going to the West Coast this particular occasion to see one of my own plays in Los Angeles and to see and make love to an old girl-friend of mine in San Francisco. People get upset when you tell them the truth, some might even be hurt, especially those who have strange stickers on the bumpers of their cars. Now, what if I had said, "I'm a playwright involved in the Black Revolution and I'm hitchhiking to California to see one of my black revolutionary plays?" Or, "I'm going to see my ex-girlfriend. She's white, you know. (Winking as I say it.) And I don't honestly know truthfully whether I'm going to see my play out there, 'cause I've seen it already, or to see her. (Smiling at my own candor.) She's very nice and white, being Jewish and raised in St. Louis, but actually born in Texas, so more than likely you have much in common with her."

Now, I couldn't say that, could I? Those answers shouldn't come from black hitchhikers, writers or no. And since I knew this, I changed my speech accordingly.

"Yeah, Patsy Mae and me are gonna have a mess of kids. Maybe six or more."

"Well boy, if you and your little lady ever get down to Lexington, I got a friend who can always use a good presser."

"Oh thanks a lot."

Night closed in on the road and the Southern Pennsylvania hills and a sign came up: WELCOME TO MARYLAND—NO HITCHHIKING!

"I thought Colorado was the only state that outlawed hitchhiking," I said.

"Well, you never know, boy, now do you?"

And his speedometer was at 95.

"Don't feel like we goin' ninety-five, do it, boy?"

"Nawh."

"Well we are. I'll have it up to a hundred and five before the night's over."

"You will, huh?"

"This is a special car, you know, boy. I guess you've guessed that by now, huh?"

"Oh, yeah, I did."

"Don't see many floor shifts like this, huh? This is a test model. That's about all I do now. Test special cars. But I used to be a truck driver."

"It must be interesting."

"Oh, it is, boy. It is."

"It seems that way."

"You ever hear of the John Birch Society, boy?"

"John Birch?"

"Yeah, the John Birch Society."

It was black outside. The road was straight and deserted ahead and winter had raped the trees that bordered and bent over us. We were in West Virginia.

"Yup. That's all I do, mostly. Just go around and check and see. My job in the New Jersey chapter of our group is to collect information. My territory is Jersey, Pennsylvania, part of Maryland and Delaware and southern New York. Sometimes I travel all weekend."

"It must be an interesting job."

"It is, boy. It is. I really work for the Ford Motor Company but I get enough time off and travel expenses to get around. This is the special car they give me. It's hopped up."

"Do they give you a new one every year?"

"No, every other. It's got a supercharger and a lot of stuff you probably never heard of."

"Yeah, that's right."

We entered Virginia and his speedometer read 110.

"Things are really getting bad," he sighed. "Commies taking over everything. You go to church, boy?"

"Oh, yes, I do. Yes, I do."

"You do, huh? What kind?"

"Baptist."

"Baptist, huh?"

"Yeah, Baptist."

"Do you know about Martin Luther King?"

"Who?"

"King! Martin Luther King . . . the freedom marcher."

"Ohhh . . ."

"Yeah, him."

"Well, I've heard about him but I ain't one of his followers."

"Good. The damned Commie. You know that's all that's behind him, don'cha?"

"Well, I don't keep up with that kinda stuff too much."

"It's just as well that you don't. It's really a mess. 'Cause when he can't get things to go as fast as how he thinks it should go he comes in, gets good colored people like you, boy, all riled up and just makes trouble. Damned Commie. That's my job—to see what's going on and to spread information. If it wasn't for groups like us I don't know how long this country would last."

"Yeah, I see what you mean."

"The Commies infest this country. From the White House on down. There's a lot of things you don't know, boy. It was a colored man in 1914 that wrote a paper describing the coming Commie take-over. He was a Commie. Way back then was when they started planning and working, the Commies, the Jews and the niggers . . . no offense to you, boy, but some of your people just act like they are."

"You come from Lexington?" I asked.

"Naw, not originally. My father teaches down there. Virginia Military Institute. He's one of those that got me first interested in our group. My dad's a real fireball. I've tried to join the service over a dozen times but they won't take me. Me with college and all, but they don't take me . . . I got ulcers."

"That's strange they won't take you and you test out these highpowered cars."

"Yeah, they thought I'd get in and cost them a lot of money. Ulcers sure are expensive. My dad's done spent over twenty thousand dollars on his in the last six years."

"Where do you drive your test cars?"

"Oh, around the country. On tracks sometimes. I race them too, you see. And I can drive anything, boy, anything that's got wheels. Drove for Smith Brothers Trucking in Virginia for years, still take out a load for them when they get pressed. Damned good outfit, and I'm studying for my pilot's license when I ain't driving."

"You gonna fly a jet?"

"Naw, helicopters. That's where the money is. Ferry around executives."

A small dish-rag grey carcass lay in the road. My driver told me it was a skunk, that skunks infested that part of the country. The temperature rose and we cracked the windows, sniffing warmer air and an occasional unfortunate skunk.

"Yeah, I was married once," the driver said. "But that didn't work. Damned American women don't want their men to be individuals anymore. Want them never to get out of high school. I don't smoke or drink and I'm a hard worker. I believe in this country, boy, and its women . . . and its men too, but I just ain't going to bed with just any tramp that comes along. I'm savin' myself for a real woman. I was reared in the seat of the Confederacy."

We entered Lexington about nine.

"Damn, this is the best time I ever drove that stretch in my life. This new highway system they putting in really gets us here. Four states in half the time. I left New York only hours ago. The good old Army's behind it. Sees the need of staying mobile and ready."

"Your father teaches college?" I asked.

"Yeah, Dad was in business a long while but the Commies and ulcers drove him out. Now he's back to what he really wants to do."

"I wish I had gone to college," I said.

"Listen, boy. I got two degrees and I can tell you that you ain't missed a damned thing, let me tell you."

He showed me the college and told me that Jefferson Davis was born in Lexington. Then he pointed out Route 60.

"Well, we just passed a Baptist church. One of yours, boy. But it's for white folks. This is the real South, you understand? It's a lot different if you never been here. Now, this is the way you go. Keep on this road out of town. I wouldn't stop and try to get a ride before I got out of town, if I was you."

"Thanks," I said.

"Oh, before I forget it." He handed me a John Birch Society pamphlet. "Don't want you to get away clean, now do I, boy?" He smiled. "I feel kinda guilty 'cause all my heavy artillery is locked in my trunk but this is enough to get you started."

"Thanks, I really appreciate it."

"Now, that's all right. Just wait 'til you get out of town before you try and get a lift. It's dark out there but it's warm."

On my way out of town, a group of five black boys passed me and each said, "Hi," when passing, and they smiled as a group.

On the edge of town, five cars passed me, one stopping so that the driver could peer at me, then accelerating with a tearing of tires, the tail lights dissolving in the night.

Five minutes later, a car stopped. The driver was heavy and black.

"Where the hell you goin'?" he said.

"West."

"How goddamn far west?"

"California."

"Get in. I'm goin' all the hell the way to Cincinnati and you goddamn better keep me awake."

"Thanks, I will."

"Don't say another word, sport. What the hell you goin' to California for? You go to school or somethin'?"

"Nawh. I'm going get married and I usually work as a janitor."

I didn't feel too bad telling him that; I have been a janitor at times and who knows, maybe one day I'll get married again.

"Well, I'm in the Army, myself, youngster. Twenty-three goddamn years' worth. Just re-enlisted and bought this brand-new Impala. Yeah, spent my leave with my girl before I go to Korea! She's eighteen, my girl, and the prettiest little thing in this man's Army. Can't see what she sees in my old ass."

"Well, Sarge, there's more to it than looks."

"Sure is, son."

"Now take my Patsy Mae for a case. I'm the family man type and I shy away from those lookers but the moment I laid eyes on Patsy Mae . . ."

And that's how it was across a lot of the country. Next time I might fly, except that there's a lot of stories to hear and see between here and there.

SUPPORT YOUR LOCAL POLICE!!!

WELCOME TO MARYLAND—NO HITCHHIKING!

SUPPORT YOUR LOCAL POLICE!!!

95 M.P.H.

SUPPORT YOUR LOCAL POLICE!!!

SPEED LIMIT IS POSTED.

SUPPORT YOUR LOCAL POLICE!!!

SLOW DOWN AND LIVE!

SUPPORT YOUR LOCAL POLICE!!!

110 M.P.H.

SUPPORT YOUR LOCAL POLICE!!!

SPEED CHECK BY RADAR

SUPPORT YOUR LOCAL POLICE!!!

END OF FREEWAY

SUPPORT YOUR LOCAL POLICE!!!

FARM LABOR INFORMATION

SUPPORT YOUR LOCAL POLICE!!!

SUPPORT YOUR LOCAL POLICE!!!

SUPPORT YOUR LOCAL POLICE!!!

DANDY, or
Astride the Funky Finger of Lust

Dedicated to Malcolm X . . .
who too wore a "zoot" suit

"We're makin' a regular country boy out'ta you, Dandy Benson," Aunt Bessie said, wiping the flour from her hands.

Dandy laughed behind her back as she stooped to shove the biscuits in the oven, and muttered "like hell" under his breath.

"What did you say?" she asked.

"Nothin'."

Dandy took his swatter and eased over in back of Marie Ann to smash the fly she was stalking.

"Git on away from here, Dandy Benson," she giggled. Her brown face burst into joy.

"This is man's work, Marie Ann," Dandy drawled.

She pulled at his wrist and they began wrestling across the floor on the far side of the great kitchen from Aunt Bessie. Marie Ann's large muscular legs strained below her shorts as the two pushed and jerked. Dandy held her tight, on the sneak, to feel her young breasts.

"You kids, you kids break that up," Aunt Bessie yelled. "Break that up, you hear me, Dandy and Marie?"

They parted with Marie getting the last tap with her swatter on Dandy's rear.

"Dandy," Aunt Bessie said. "I want you to stay away from Marie," the middle-aged woman said for at least the hundredth time, Dandy thought. "You two are together too much and if anything happens to that girl, Dandy Benson, I'm going to see that somebody goes to jail and that goes for you too."

Dandy and Marie had heard Aunt Bessie's threats before; they had heard them as a regular part of their long summer days together; their being caught in childish play each day was almost routine, or the near miss of being discovered kissing or hugging, and then the following mock violence of the confrontation by the old lady they both loved. Even if they had been guilty, if Dandy were so fortunate as to be fully worthy of her suspicions, and the woman carried out her promises, they both knew that they would continue loving Aunt Bessie as nearly everyone did.

Aunt Bessie claimed love as her own, and in this manner she took the children of the poor and wretched and overworked into her warmth. She took those who would love her most.

Dandy looked out one of the windows surrounding the kitchen and wished that he had opportunity to test Aunt Bessie's threats.

Times were better now, he thought. There was so much more for him to like his second summer in Mary's Shore, Maryland. He liked the way the tan and brown of the sand and mud roads wound through the dried weed fields and meadows more this summer than his first lonely year, and he liked the animals; the dozen ducks, the eight pigs, the horse, Jim, and the couple hundred chickens that Aunt Bess and Uncle Clyde kept on their sixteen-acre farm. He even kind of liked Uncle Clyde, a little bit at least, and surely the second summer's entire bunch better than the ones of his first vacation in Maryland. Even the year before that first one in Eastern Shore, spent in New Jersey with his near-white Aunt Martha, there wasn't the same dismal emptiness as the vacation of the first year with Aunt Bessie, even though there was no one in New Jersey with him but Aunt Martha and her maid, cook and handyman who doubled at driving the shiny new black Buick and was called "the chauffeur."

The first summer with Aunt Bessie, the kids had been either too young or all from the same little town of Chester, Pennsylvania, except him, and Dandy couldn't stomach much of their attempting to convert the freedom of Aunt Bess's farm into an extension of little Chester.

But this year there was Roy Howes, and there were Jack, Marie Ann and Richard Bowen. And there was Ida.

Aunt Bessie boarded out kids for the state adoption, correction and welfare agencies, and in the summer she and Uncle Clyde took in additional summer guests from the city. Dandy was from Philadelphia—that's why they had begun calling him Dandy, from his jitterbug clothes he arrived in, and his cool impractical walk which was difficult to show on the soft dirt roads in his snake-skinned, pointy-toed shoes he had to abandon for loafers; but he still hadn't altogether dropped the strut because he *knew* the city had made him to be different from the other boys there in that farm land.

"Go out and empty the garbage, Dandy," Aunt Bessie said. "Uncle Clyde and Jack and the little boys will be home soon."

That was a job that Dandy did well. He enjoyed the pull the bucket gave his muscles when he lifted the tin container and carried the swishing mess outside and across the yard to the pig barrel. The two dogs, a young German shepherd named Pudgy, and a collie, Cisco, always followed him across the yard begging him to drop them a scrap or throw them crusts as he sometimes did.

A wooden cover was on the barrel and Dandy had to slide it off with one hand while holding the bucket high so the dogs would not poke their snouts in and drag garbage around the yard and later get sick, having their stomach's contents heaved up, drawing flies. Whenever Aunt Bessie cleaned chickens she especially warned Dandy, for one day Pudgy poked his head in the slop bucket quickly and pulled out a long chicken gut tied together with other chicken guts, and the shepherd and Cisco had dragged the garbage about the yard while several chickens, who had slipped under their fence and constantly ran the yard, chased after the scraps the dogs dropped and tore off. The hens pecked furiously away at the raw meat as if they didn't know they were devouring their brothers, and Aunt Bessie had gotten ill.

So with care Dandy lifted the bucket and sluiced the contents into the mixture. He stood and watched as the large pieces floated to the top and then were sucked under in the crawling stew, while air bubbles burped and the mess stirred internally and gave off yeasty sounds and sourer smells. The dogs' whines did not even muffle the popping of the pigs' pudding.

Dandy stood just off the driveway which half-mooned around the house and cut the yard in two pushing the workrooms, barn and hen house into the background. The slop barrel hunkered beside an old wooden truck trailer that had been mounted on cinder blocks to the right of the house. Uncle Clyde used the trailer for a tool room and stored his pig and chicken feed in its cool wooden gloom.

The horse compound, stall, barn and hen house with a shabby assortment of several other buildings formed a broken-toothed back wall to the yard. In front of the hen house grew a tree with swing hanging from its lower branches. Dandy remembered the first summer when there were two little dark girls with the whitest of whites in their eyes to swing on the empty swing. He turned back and put the top back upon the barrel. In back of the barn and hen house and buildings was the manure pile, and down a small hill to ground spongy wet in the autumn rains, was the pigpen with four large pigs in one half of the compound and four little porkers on the other side. Dandy would feed them after supper when it began to get dark and cool.

Behind the pigpen were woods for a quarter of a mile and behind the trees were the church camp grounds; every year in August the Mary's Shore colored community gave an ole timey camp meetin'. Mary's Shore was in fact a town two miles away, two country miles, but where Aunt Bessie's farm sat was closer to the crossing of Mt. Holy. Three roads converged like blinded snakes; the road from Hamilton, the twisted and adventurous route from Bicksley, and the Biltmore dust highway. On one corner was a store with an ancient filling pump, an old-style one with gauges in the head and the liquid moving down the glass bulb like bubbling sand in an hourglass. On the other corner was Sister Ossie Mae Hewett's house and land. And at the apex of the triangle was the Mt. Holy Methodist church. Opposite Aunt Bessie's field, running a quarter mile toward the crossing, was the Mt. Holy cemetery. The small settlement of black farmers and laborers was more often called by themselves Mt. Holy than anything else.

"You sho drag feet, Dandy Wandy," Marie Ann said when he entered the kitchen. She tickled the back of his head with the fly swatter as he went past. Aunt Bessie was again bent over the oven. She was a large-boned, heavy-fleshed woman who eternally laughed and joked, showing her flashy store teeth. She was very proud of her teeth, almost as proud of them as she was of herself. Dandy thought that the way she managed things and worked the love and affection from people was like a pimp who psychs out his whores. She was a shrewd extrovert with a heart big enough to satisfy even herself. But Dandy knew her, knew she believed in nothing, as he did, not even in the God she went in search of three times a week at the whitewashed church up the road, for she was what Dandy called a phoney, though she was nice, one of his favorite people of all those he knew, so he liked her very much while not trusting her a bit.

"Why, here they come," Aunt Bessie exclaimed in her booming voice. "Here come my boys."

An old Packard groaned around the driveway and halted. The front passenger door opened and a tall dark young man stepped out and turned away from the house and headed for the outhouse. From the rear doors skipped a brown laughing boy and a thin dark one circled the car to join the other.

"Hey, hey, Fatso," the brown boy screamed in mirth as the dogs pranced and yapped about him.

"Ahhh, Roy, you better not tell," the darker one said. "Ahhh . . . Roy."

"Heee hee heee . . . Oooooo man," the brown boy laughed and began running around the car with the dark one after him, the dogs completing the circle.

"Git on in the house and get ready fo dinner," the man in the car said. He sat in his driver's place and shouted through the window.

The two boys came in the house letting the screen door bang behind them.

"You little boys stop lettin' that screen door bang," Marie Ann shouted.

"Oh, shut up, girl," one of them said.

"Wait, wait . . . before you two little boys get ready for supper I want you to walk up to Sister Ossie Mae Hewett's where Ida is workin'," Aunt Bessie said.

"Yes, Aunt Bessie," the dark boy said.

"Walk home with Ida and Sister Ossie's goin' ta send back some tomatoes and peaches."

"Hee . . . hee . . ." Roy chortled.

"Didn't you hear Aunt Bess, boy?" Marie Ann asked. "What's wrong with you little boys?"

"But Aunt Bess . . . hee hee," Roy tried to choke out, but his laugh bent him over near to the floor.

"Look at that silly boy," Aunt Bessie said, her face cracking into a smile for the joke that had to come.

"What's wrong with that boy?" Marie Ann wanted to know.

"Don't listen to him, Aunt Bessie," Richard said. "He's tryin' ta make fun ah me. Don't listen ta him, Aunt Bess."

"Aunt Bess, Fatso . . . he . . . he," Roy began, pointing at the thin boy, "he tried . . . heee hee heeee."

"I don't want to hear about Richard Bowen," Aunt Bessie blustered when Roy stretched out on the floor and sobbed with mirth. "Get on up to Sister Ossie Mae's and get Ida."

The boys left finally with Richard grabbing a slim stick from the woodshed in back of the trailer and crying "Oooo man" and chasing Roy around the drive and out in front of the house and up the road with the old man's shouts from the car all the while warning that they better get about their little businesses.

Dandy was helping Marie Ann set the table when the tall youth came in and slammed the screen door.

"There's mah big son," Aunt Bess said and shuddered when the door flew shut. "How did it go today, son?"

"Awlright, Aunt Bessie," he said, deepening his voice on purpose to a musical baritone.

"How's my big bro' Bowen," Marie Ann said, pushing herself against the youth to make him lean sideways.

"What cha doin' dere, *Maurey*," the boy slipped into a playful drawl and began pushing her across the floor.

"Bo, stop pushin' your little sister," Marie Ann giggled. She tried to tickle him as they jostled their way across the room.

"Dandy, come and pull this here girl offen me," Jack called.

"No, Dandy, don't you dare, Dandy," Marie screamed, laughing as she acted like she was about to be raped. "Help me, please help me, Dandy," she pleaded.

"I'm neutral," Dandy called out, watching their mock battle, seeing the sinews bulge in Marie Anne's legs and her solid behind below the narrow waist fight the material of the shorts.

"Dandy, you better help out one of them or ole Aunt Bessie's gonna jump in to even it up," the old woman teased and began rolling up imaginary sleeves and wetting her thumbs on tongue as she threw up her dukes.

Dandy ran to the sink and pulled a damp towel from the rack and twirled it tight three times and ran across to the squirming couple and popped the towel on the seat of Marie Ann's shorts.

"Ohh . . . Dandy, you dirty dog," she whimpered.

And he popped her again, a loud and cracking whack.

"That's for the fly swatter, Marie," he said.

"Hey, what you kids doin' in dere?" the man in the car called in.

"See here, your Uncle Clyde is goin' to get you," Aunt Bess said and moved over to the door, blocking the man's view.

"Jack Bowen, you go and clean up," she said.

The couple parted.

"Just don't worry so much about inside of here when you ain't in, Clyde," Aunt Bessie hollered. "Just don't stick your nose in so much," she said to the old man in the old Packard.

"I'll be stickin' mah foot somewhere if'en I don't git some peace around here," the man in the car said.

* * *

When Jack let Marie loose, Dandy spun around with the girl swinging at him. When they were inside the front room he let her catch him and she slapped at his grinning face until they began kissing. Aunt Bessie called her to finish setting the table.

Dandy didn't want to go back into the kitchen with his just having gotten kissed and then suddenly having to act like nothing had happened. He didn't know if he could be normal.

That time at Doris's he hadn't been normal, and he had really tried that time. No matter how he tried it always betrayed him. In fact, he knew it was *he* who betrayed himself.

He had met Doris at school. She was in his home-room class and Doris had been pretty hard to miss. She was the oldest of either girls or boys for having been put away in reform school for almost three years and she was also the largest and loudest.

Doris was evil to his way of thinking . . . a type of evil which fascinated him. Not only did she curse like she wanted, she did everything else she wanted. She threatened the boys in class as well as the girls, but it was especially the boys she had made fear her, and she didn't just bluff. Of course there was probably bluster in her statements to the boys that she could cut or pull their "things" off if they messed with her or got in her way but most believed her, for she had been known to scratch girls up and hit the boys so hard on their arms and in the chest that they swore she hit like a man. Most fourteen-year-olds have not been struck by a man's full punch, but Doris's rep was secure.

Somehow she never bothered Dandy before they became friends. For all of Dandy's swagger, essentially he
was a quiet boy. After school he would go home and
work on his motor bike, or hopelessly unable to find a
defect, he and his friend Homer would take a ride or
go by some girl's house. Homer lived next door to him
and they were the only two in their neighborhood who
had motor bikes. Dandy had gotten his by begging his
mother for two long weeks. Homer had gotten his six
weeks later by taking an extra job after school. Some
days Dandy didn't ride with Homer nor tamper with his
bike's efficiency. He went around the corner to the 8th
Street gym in the basement of the police station. There
he trained for the future. That's what he thought he
would be some day, a fighter.

Columbia Avenue in North Philly in some of its neon
stretches has a bar at every corner and one, two or
three in between. It is a street of pawnshops, trolley
cars, pimps, markets, jazz, real-estate offices, hustlers,
the hustled, lawyers, whores, junkies, blues, and more
blues and bars and movies—the main artery of a ghetto,
Dandy's neighborhood.

Up north, in the city, Dandy was mostly called Stevie. And the Saturday afternoon that Stevie Benson
and Homer met Snoopy and his boys, the Avenue was
jumpin', a drunk's delight and a cock-hound's carnival.
Stevie and Homer had crossed Broad and passed the
five-and-ten when they were stopped by five boys who
stepped from the alley next to the show.

"Hey, what's happenin', man?" the dark wiry leader
said to Stevie.

"How's it goin', Homer?" one of the boys said to Stevie's friend.

"What the fuck is this supposed to be, man?" Homer asked. Homer was older than any of them and the boys in front of him grinned and backed off. Stevie didn't know any of the gang.

"I said what's happenin'," the leader spoke again.

"Nothin', what's happen'n' with you, man?" Stevie replied.

No one else spoke. Homer strolled to the curb and sat on the bumper of a car. The other boys faded aside, leaving the pair alone.

"How 'bout loanin' me a nickel, man?" the leader said.

"I ain't got it."

"Ain't cha goin'nin' da movie?"

"Yeah."

"Den wha'cha mean ya ain't got it? All I find I can have?" He reached toward Stevie's pocket.

Stevie stepped back into a fighting stance and shoved the boy's hand aside. From the edges of his eyes shapes moved.

"Don't worry 'bout yore back," Homer said. "This is just between you and him."

"What are ya supposed to be . . . bad, man?" the leader asked Stevie.

"Bad enough, man."

"I'll see ya 'round," he said and he and his boys stepped back into the alley, glaring as they retreated.

There were three fights that afternoon in the movies. Two between rival gangs and one in the balcony between two gassed head dudes over a girl who left with a third fellow. Homer told Stevie how well he had done with Snoopy and they stayed out of hassles for the remainder of that day.

The rest of the weekend was spent with Homer instructing Stevie in what to look for and how to face it, for trouble was surely coming.

Monday morning was like many others. The dreary succession of junior high school classes passed with the same amount of perverse violence by the students and the exact amount of hate that big city slum schoolteachers can radiate. The erasers were thrown at Wild Leo in the third row by the hysterical, horn-rimmed redhead who taught something she said was social functioning; the zigging chalk whistled down the aisle at some pompadoured head in math class; the spitball that splattered upon the neck of the shellshocked English teacher caused him to verbally fornicate with Jesus; the dragging of Pancho the Spic down to the principal's office for writing obscene suggestions to Rita the Jew; the accumulated deadening hate of packing fifty-one haters in a space that only thirty could possibly fit—Monday morning was like many others.

In this school Stevie had to hide always, had to hide his intelligence from teachers as well as students. He had to hide his willingness to learn, his wanting to know and find out. But now, in his second year, he knew how to hide. In his first he was green and had found himself in fights each week; sometimes three or four in a gang would beat him up as he fought back wildly like a caged animal that didn't have instinct enough to run, even if the gate was opened. These fights usually ended when they hit him in the eyes, blinding him, and then pounded and kicked him to the ground as an added treat to the hundreds of schoolmates jeering the loser.

Force was what the crowd worshipped, Stevie learned. And for all the many good fights he had provided the mob, hardly anybody acknowledged him as a fighter. Losers are not often kept in mind as long as a year. And there had been no fight for Stevie for over a year, since he had learned to hide so well.

After the lunch hour, the kids formed lines to march back into classroom. Stevie waited in his line, behind the numerous heads, not thinking of the long afternoon hours ahead, only sucking at the scraps of baloney caught between his teeth, from the king-sized hoagie he had eaten at the little lunch counter on Fifth Street.

"Hey, mahthafukker!" a voice at his side said loudly.

Stevie turned his head to see as did the rest of the kids; it was Snoopy.

"I'll be waitin' fo ya after school, ya little punk," Snoopy warned. "Don't try and git away."

A steady drone teased Stevie's ears the remainder of the afternoon. Guys and girls he didn't know stared at him and pointed and giggled. Some made pantomimed gestures—a boney fist smashing his mouth and the bugged-eyed expression of the punchdrunk, a mighty dig to the gut with a boloed right and the resulting doubling up and retching. The mood was intensifying for the afternoon's pagan dance.

Those who knew Stevie turned their heads or stayed far from him. Two friends from his neighborhood, his age, Brother and Timmy, looked knowingly and smiled and nodded among themselves, sharing this one more defeat of Stevie whom they had known and seen defeated many other times. A few girls told him how sorry they were and for him to run out the side exit when the bell rang, or even before school ended. Who was Snoopy to create this total terror, he wondered. Stevie was out of his neighborhood, with no strong neighborhood friends to side with him, and had always been an outcast and foreigner during his school life because the schools closest to him were so "bad" his mother threatened him with boarding school if he were ever compelled to go by the authorities. He constantly lied about his address. So, he had nobody there but himself. The Jewish boys he knew and the several Irish, Italian and Polish guys wouldn't mix in a fight among Negroes even if one of them was a friend and the other a stranger with a gang to back him up. Fear of the gang was one more reason why he couldn't ask his few friends.

Toward the end of the last period, Stevie raised his hand and asked to be excused from class. A tittering rustle rose about him as he got up and left the room. Inside the boy's toilet his stomach knotted as he sat on the john and tried to think of nothing and keep his legs from trembling, and after a while he straightened his clothes and in the mirror above the washbowl he feinted his left like Homer had shown him over the weekend and shadow-boxed a barrage of hooks and uppercuts into his imaginary opponent's surprised face. He then danced back, waiting for his dream adversary's vicious counterattack but stopped him cold with a low right hand thrown belt-high as he charged in flailing, and Stevie finally creamed the shadow to the sidewalk with a left bolo to the kidneys. Before he left the cement room he pissed at the urinal, shaking the last drops into his palms and massaging the moist skin for luck.

"Little sucker, you gonna git your ass stomped *today*," Doris said, and he saw the joy of his return on his classmates' faces. "Fool, you should'a got away when ya had the chance," the big girl said when they lined up to leave school.

The fall sky was as grey as a morgue slab, and a pagan dance was held that day, a dance that marked the end and the beginning of something for Stevie Benson. The mob awaited the initiation, jostling and shoving to get better places. All the whites hurried home except for a few from over by the freight yards and from down the waterfront.

When Stevie came out his firetower exit, two boys bigger than he broke through the line and fell in step with him.

Doris ran up behind.

"Let me hold your coat," she screamed above the gleeful mob.

Stevie pulled his jacket off and put it under his arm.

"Let me hold your coat, little sucker . . . you can't fight with a coat!"

He gave it to her. For blocks they walked, blocks of emptied streets except for Stevie, his two escorts, Doris and the two hundred jostling figures. No one over eighteen stepped from a door; not a teacher or coach or administrator was seen seeking out his car or slinking to a bus stop that day until the dancers upon the concrete were blocks away, souls in time to the trotting and trucking of the savage song of the threshing floor.

Wild Leo screamed and whooped, pushing Pancho the Spic and grabbing leering Rita's hair. Black Delores, her face like a sooted Madonna with white rolling eyes, cried real tears, letting the streaks run over her lovely face like rain tracks upon coal. She stayed near but turned away and cried whenever Stevie glanced at her. Brother and Timmy, on the edges of the mob, smirked and stared straight at him when they got their chance.

The parade crossed Eighth Street, then Darien and at last Ninth waited with a vacant gravel lot across the street from the train bridge. Snoopy squatted there sifting the grit through his fingers with at least ten street fighters around him.

"Dis is gonna be a fair fight, mahthafukker," Snoopy said when he rose and met the party. "I'm gonna kick yore ass until yore nose bleeds, punk." He took off his Eisenhower jacket and shrugged his shoulders to ripple his muscles. "You'll beg yore mamma to give you money ta bring ta me, ya understand!"

Stevie remained quiet. A burly boy with a greasy green tam pulled down over his conked head acted as referee. Cheers and squeals rose among the crowd as the referee gave instructions, and pairs of anxious boys began body-punching, the thuds and whacks beating out until the real fight began. Delores stood high on a stoop down the street, framed in the door, as alone as Stevie. Two bobby-socked girls picked up Snoopy's jacket and were on the verge of having a preliminary until the smaller backed down.

The referee pointed to Stevie. "When I say break, punk, you better scratch ass and git back like I tell you or you'll git yore little ass stomped today as well as whupped."

The two came to the center of the circle and began dancing like lightweights. Stevie was indeed an amateur lightweight but had only sparred with the boys in his neighborhood and the club fighters who used the police equipment on weekends. Snoopy's twenty-pound weight-edge and his three year advantage caused him to close fast with Stevie. Stevie won the first exchange by giving the clumsier boy two glancing jolts in the face with his left and right; Snoopy's swing swooshed above the little guy's head. They closed again, immediately, and Stevie tied up his opponent in a clinch and pumped quick shots to the kidneys and gut as he had been taught. Surprised and ashamed at the crowd's wild cheers for the underdog, Snoopy tried to butt him but Stevie had been waiting and dug his head into the taller boy's chest, making him smash his nose. As they broke Stevie hit Snoopy again upon his bloodied nose. And the referee stepped in.

"Here, man," he screamed, talking to Snoopy, "let me take this mahthafukker." He had pulled his sweater off in the late fall weather, and Snoopy stood between him and Stevie as the mob surged out into the street.

"No, no, no, man," Snoopy pleaded. "I can take him. I CAN TAKE THIS LITTLE PUNK ANYTIME I WANT!"

The rest of the gang whispered among themselves, but Snoopy wouldn't listen to them when they stepped into the circle with the mob at their heels.

"C'mon, man," Snoopy said to Stevie, pushing his friends back. "It's you and me now, little mahthafukker."

Stevie knew it was his fight and didn't think of anything but winning. No more hiding, no more pulling punches and not talking to the girls at school because he was out of his neighborhood. No more copping out and eating shit. No more, no more! They came for the dance, so now for the floor show. I'm the best, he told himself; I'm the best and today we all find out.

The ring cleared with even the referee pulled out and Stevie bobbed and weaved as he pressed in on the dark boy, something he hadn't done before. He jabbed Snoopy four times quickly around the arms and chest and landed once in the throat. He danced, he danced so beautifully, he knew, like to music, like to the sound of drums and clashing cymbals. There was no other place in the universe then for him but that dance floor with every fiber poised and executing an ageless war dance passed down from his father and his father's father before him and the black fathers of his tribe before memory. He danced back, letting Snoopy's swing slip past and then feinted with his left. Snoopy blinked and then stepped . . . the gang leader woke up six minutes later with a busted mouth and nose; one eye would be closed shut for two days, and his head would ache for a time because of the mild concussion he received when his skull cracked the curb. Stevie had stood above him for a second after the feint and vicious combination of one, two, three and more jabs pumped into the big boy's face, and then the overhand right, and the step behind the pivot and the hook which smashed into flesh and bone.

He waited for the fallen boy's counterattack.

"Here, mahthafukker," Doris screamed in the stunned second. "Run, mahthafukker, run . . . RUN!"

Stevie took his coat thrown at him and sped through the crowd behind him, speeding past smiling pearly-toothed Delores, running down the hill toward home. Running like he had never run in his life. All of Snoopy's boys seemed to be fifty steps behind, and behind them was the insane mob, crazy from the smash performance and lusting for added gore.

At the corner, an old Hudson turned and Stevie grabbed the door handle and leaped inside.

"What the hell?" the driver started, but the exhausted boy pointed back and one look through the rearview mirror gave the driver incentive to tramp on the gas.

After a week of negotiations between Homer and Snoopy and missing days at school with a couple of running fights between Snoopy's boys and the ones Homer sent to escort Stevie back to his territory, the thing settled, and Brother and Timmy said: "You won!" and nodded their heads as they passed.

The following week Doris took Stevie to her house after school and ordered her little brother out. Then she showed Stevie how to really have sex, the way grown-ups did.

They met at her place every day after school for over a month. She told him about the other big guys she had at night, real men, she said, some even fathers and husbands that she had whenever she wanted. It seemed to Stevie that it was always she who wanted them from her way of telling it, and refused if they made demands upon her. She lived on the top floor of a tenement and one day when Stevie was between her large dark thighs, his teeth nibbling at her earlobe the way she had showed him as they grunted and strained, they heard a loose step crack. He jumped up and ran to the window and Doris pulled down her dress just as her girlfriend pushed the door open and walked in.

"Don't ya know how to knock, bitch?" Doris growled.

"I've never had to before . . . was I interruptin' somethin'?" the girl asked. She was taller than Doris and almost as old. She was a grade ahead of both Stevie and Doris, and she and Doris ran around with a gang that called themselves The Controlerellas.

"How are you, Chuckie?" the girl asked Stevie. In this part of town he had a different nickname.

"Okay," he said over his shoulder.

He watched out the window. His fly had been buttoned just in time but the front of his pants pushed out. He peered from the window as the girls talked, watching the trolley and cars go down Tenth Street, and the people on the streets that day, and looking south he saw the tall P.S.F.S. building, rising from the grey dust of the slums, towering above them as if the structure's foundation was planted in the muck of the ghetto.

The street below looked small to Stevie and innocent, but he knew it was one of the main trails in the jungle. He liked being up high looking down at the people. He liked being there with Doris, even though she bullied him in public; she was nice to him when they were alone, and best of all she said she liked the way he did it to her because he was young and strong and it took him a long time to finish.

"Give me a cigarette, Chuck," Doris's friend said.

He turned his head away from the window; she was smiling.

"Give me a cigarette, boy!"

He walked over to the couch and handed her a ciga-rette from his pack. She shrieked with laughter as she snatched it and leaned across Doris, choking and cough-ing. Stevie peeped down at his pants front.

He always betrayed himself, he knew. Always.

"Give me one too," Doris said. She snatched the en-tire pack from his hands. "You don't need any, you silly little bastard."

Her friend laughed even louder.

Doris let him come to see her two more afternoons, but the times after that day of discovery when he asked to be let up her stairs, she told him no, though sometimes she would let him kiss her hurriedly in her vestibule. She stopped coming to school and the kids gossiped that she had been thrown out because of being pregnant.

The week before she died Stevie and Homer were on Hutchinson Street, close to where Doris lived. They waited outside a girl's house who they were going to walk back to their neighborhood for a party. As they waited Doris walked through the narrow streets with her tall, thin friend.

"Hey, lil' mahthafukker," she yelled to Stevie, "what-cha doin' up this way?" She stopped, placing her hands on over-blown hips, and stared at him through shiny eyes. "You know we don't allow little pricks up here."

She was loud and evil-sounding like the times at school when she threatened the boys, so Stevie knew she wasn't serious.

"Just hangin' out," he answered.

"Whatcha been doin' lately?" she asked.

"Just eatin' fried chicken and fukkin' ev'va night, baby," he said, saying the line of the street song with a smile.

The girls flounced off in hobbling skirts and jeered at him to get out of "their" territory and swung their behinds in huge circles down the street, laughing, stumbling and swearing.

"Whatcha let that whore speak ta ya like that fo, man?" Homer had said. "You should'a punched that black bitch in da mouf."

Dandy had never told anyone about Doris. She had been his first, the first that mattered, for he had been playing sex games among the tenements since he was seven, but Doris had been the one who had made him feel for the first time that something which frightened and was vital to him. The only times before the quick afternoons with Doris on her couch was when he had had dreams he couldn't make out but he awoke afterwards on his belly, wet and scared.

Since the first day with Doris he had sought out at least ten other girls. Slum girls who waited for any show of affection, especially from one their own age with a smooth brown face and who knew what to do. Dandy's challenge to Doris hadn't been entirely groundless, even though sweet black Delores would only let him love her from across the aisle. He was out in the street every night. He knew Doris wanted to see him after the encounter on the side street, and her boisterous smile made him sweat some as he promised to go see her, for his feelings for the girl had grown suddenly proportional to his pants front which moved out as he thought of her luscious warmth. He didn't make it to her place that week. The next, Doris died shortly after missing a fire net drawn under the window of her burning apartment.

Dandy stopped by to see her little brother some weeks later and they both whispered of her and cried without thinking of being manly.

". . . And by the grace of God . . . Ahhhmen," Uncle Clyde intoned.

"Pass the biscuits," Roy said.

"Just wait a minute, boy," Richard ordered and acted cross and older than he was. "Shouldn't be so greedy!"

"Hush up you two little boys," Ida James said. "All the way back from Sister Ossie Mae's you been at it."

"Yeah, keep quiet, you little boys," Uncle Clyde said with a mouth filled with food.

"Here, Dandy," Ida said and poured his lemonade for him.

"Why looky dere . . . old Dandy's makin' out like a madman," Jack Bowen slurred.

"Marie Ann, ya better look out or Ida will be takin' Dandy away from you," Roy said.

Marie shrugged and shoveled a spoonful of beans into her mouth. "Nobody's studden 'bout Dandy."

"Dandy, your city ways don't seem to be workin' any on Marie Ann," Aunt Bessie said. "What's wrong, boy?" She prodded Dandy, for she knew that he was working on her favorite and he would have her if he got the chance.

"I don't know," Dandy answered. "I guess she thinks I'm a slicker."

"Hee hee heee . . ." Roy chortled. "Oooeee . . . hee heee . . ."

"Eat your supper, boy!"

"Well, that's what you is, boy," Jack drawled and slipped tenses and syntax. "One of dem dere city slickers, and mah lil sister ain'ta gonna be fooled none any by y'all kind, *boy*." He made a private joke, though secretly he wanted his sister and Dandy to be friendlier. Dandy would make a pretty fair brother-in-law, he thought, and he felt that any man who ever touched her would *have* to marry Marie Ann.

"Why are you so quiet, Sister Ida?" Uncle Clyde asked.

"Not much ta say, Unc' Clyde."

Ida was a stocky yellow girl who had been turned out by her mother after her father had taken her for over a period of two years and at last had succeeded in giving her his son. She was a ward of the state from being a minor and for having made herself available to any man in her town, forty miles south of Mary's Shore, who had the courage to talk to the fifteen-year-old for over five minutes. Many had the guts and word finally got around to the authorities that a girl and baby were living in an abandoned shack, close to town, and there were all sorts of carryings-on. The powers couldn't charge Ida with anything more than vagrancy since she never asked for money from her numerous visitors, and not even vag stuck when it was found she was a teen-ager, though she seemed ten years older, or so it was assumed. Ida didn't talk much and Dandy suspected that she was a bit dense since she was relieved that her baby had been taken from her. But she had enough sense to slip him a note his first day there that her heart was just about to actually burst from love of him.

She worked each day on a neighboring farm watching children or helping in the kitchen, for at least one member of each family in Mt. Holy had to go into town or farther to jobs in outlying districts. Some drove even to Dover and to Wilmington in Delaware.

Dandy knew his turn would come with Ida. Jack had told him how he would get her when he had the chance, not knowing that Dandy also schemed on her stubby flanks, for they both were sure that Ida James was as hot and ready as a ten-cent pistol.

"Dandy," Uncle Clyde asked, "when you comin' out with me or one of the boys on the job?"

"Anytime, Uncle Clyde, how 'bout tomorrow?"

"Clyde, you know that boy don't want to work," Aunt Bessie said. She rubbed it in about Dandy being able to pay his board without working, for Dandy's mother had a civil-service job in the city, and the city slick Dandy was from Philly and had taken piano lessons and boxing lessons and singing and dancing lessons, and had a motorcycle (really only a motor bike). He was her current status symbol.

"No, he probably can't pull himself away from Marie Ann," Ida said and peeped over her fork at the other girl across the table.

"I wish he could go somewheres," Marie Ann said. "I'm sure tired of lookin' at him."

The remainder of the table, except for Uncle Clyde, entered the conversation and bet about which of the girls would get Dandy, and the dinner ended with Aunt Bess promising that if anybody got Marie Ann they would go immediately to jail, whether or not they used "protection."

"NOW, BESSIE, YOU KNOW YOU SHOULDN'T BE TALKIN' LIKE DAT IN FRONT OF DESE HARE KIDS," Uncle Clyde hollered, nearly upsetting his greens.

"Well, all of them are big enough to take care of themselves, and none of mine ain't goin' 'round dumb for most of their lives, especially about somethin' that everybody has got ta do . . . or at least should try once, Clyde."

"Oh, hush up, woman."

"Well, I've told them already and even given them money to get 'em with," the old woman said. "All they have ta do is come and ask and I'll give them money to buy them. I ain't takin' the blame if somethin' happens. I'll tell the world it ain't Bessie's fault."

"You talk too much, Bessie."

It was a good dinner.

After dinner, Dandy went to the trailer and poured hog feed into two large slop buckets and then carried them outside to the pig barrel. Setting them down, he lifted the large ladle and began filling the buckets, a scoop at a time. The dogs had been tied for their evening feed, given by Roy coaxing and wheedling with puckered lips and many "Here boys" to the already leashed animals. As Dandy started on the second bucket Marie Ann and Ida came out of the house and they tugged at each other until one got the last tag; then Marie began trotting over toward the hen house where the outhouse stood.

"I'm goin' to get you when ya come back, Marie Ann," Ida called out.

"Ya know what you'll git, Ida," she said, turning around and making a fist and showing where on the light girl's face she would plant it. "And that goes double for your friend Dandy," she said before she entered the closet-like building.

Ida skipped over to the trailer and went inside. Dandy submerged the edge of the ladle in the thick broth and pulled it out with sucking sounds, pouring the mixture in the nearly filled last bucket. He heard the cracked corn rattling in the pan Ida used to feed the chickens.

"Come here, Dandy, I want ta show ya somethin'," she said from inside the trailer.

Dandy saw Roy cross the yard from the horse compound, and he stirred the pigs' food until the boy was gone into the house.

"Dandy?"

Inside the trailer he found Ida in a dim corner and kissed her thick moist lips.

"I told Marie Ann that I loved you and she got mad."

"No, she didn't. You know that she likes Junior Kane."

"She did so get mad."

"She was teasin' you."

"No, she weren't and she better not!"

"We better go," Dandy said after a while. "Someone will be out here looking for us."

"Okay. I have ta go ta choir rehearsal tonight but I want ta talk ta ya when I git back."

Marie Ann was humming a hymn when Dandy passed the back of the outhouse with the heavy buckets.

The pigs were always ready to feed. No matter how Dandy filled their troughs to brimming, when he returned the next day, all had been swilled up and nothing remained but the stained, weathered boards of the troughs. When he turned the buckets up and splashed the food into the troughs, the pigs made oinking sounds which he had never gotten used to. He watched the fat beasts feeding, pushing each other aside, and remembered the story he had read of a man who had lain helpless in a pigpen and had been eaten alive.

On the way back to the house, climbing the stubbled trail beside the nearly grown summer corn, he saw three buzzards carried through the sky in the streams of invisible forces which he had been told were air currents. He found Jack Bowen waiting for him halfway up the rise.

"Well, howdy dowdy, Bowen?"

"Well, how yawhl doin', Mr. Benson?"

Jack was four years older than Dandy, but he allowed the younger boy to carry on rituals and treated him as an equal.

"How the girls treatin' ya, Bowen?" Dandy asked.

"Dey ain't treatin' one bit, partner, not a'tall."

Jack Bowen was more intelligent than Dandy; if he could break away from the farm and the series of mill-hand, packing-plant helper jobs, he could be saved, Dandy knew but could not tell his friend. Jack lived as much for the future as for payday; he was forever participating in national contests that promised trips to Paris and mink coats and an occasional Cadillac. He purposely exaggerated his drawl, though he could speak better than Dandy could then; he could tell stories like nobody else, and knew more about science, math and those subjects' vocabularies. Dandy had never heard Jack's actual plans except once.

* * *

It was a day in early July that Jack took Dandy to the chicken plant to get a job. Buddy Henderson drove them across the state line into Delaware where he and his girl worked. Buddy's girl, Betty Sue, was from Florida and chewed tobacco and wore men's pants because she had done so much field work she didn't "rightly take to dresses no mo'," and she couldn't read nor write much aside her name, Betty Sue. She had been living since spring in the shack village of itinerant workers behind the Hamilton tomato packing plant, until Buddy had gotten her to housekeep with him.

The foreman hired everyone that day, for truckloads of birds waited to be slaughtered.

Dandy's job was to hang the chickens by their feet, pulling them from the crates as they flapped, squawked and pecked, attaching the victims to metal clamps swinging under the conveyor. The belt ran, one clamp which had to be filled after another, and two farm boys worked beside Dandy and showed him how inadequate he was at hanging chickens at six bits an hour.

Sitting in a chair, ten feet down the line from Dandy, was an old fat man who cut the chickens' white throats. The man was black and wore a black rubber apron; the bib shielded his chest, the straps climbed up over his white-shirted shoulders and blended like dark bands with his neck. Dandy emptied crate after crate of white leghorns and sent them cackling down to the busy man with the blade. Sometimes a brown bird or a black with grey and white speckles found its way among the snowy ones and they added contrast, floating upended toward the chair, their red wattles dangling, then the brief last scream as one black hand reached out and anchored the head, and then the other hand moved, bringing red of a more alive hue streaming over their throats.

That lunch hour Dandy sat with Jack and Buddy Henderson and Betty Sue, eating homemade sandwiches of baloney and peanut butter.

"Hope ta gawd dese hare chickens hold out another two munts," Buddy remarked.

"I wouldn't care none if'in dey cut every last one's of da sonsabitches' throats nex' hour," Jack said. "There ain't no future bein' a chicken-plucker."

"Beats not eatin'," Buddy said. "Whatcha do if dere were no job in da chicken plant nor any in da 'maters or any work a'tall?"

"Well, I don't know 'bout chauw, Buddy boy," Jack drawled, "but one ah dese hare days I'm hoppin' dat old Greyhound out on da road an' goin' up ta Philly an' git me ah job in da big post office up dere."

"Sheet, nigger," Betty Sue said. "When's de last time ya ev'va seen some nigger in a white shirt in da post office? Dey got jest de job fo all ya white-shirt niggers right here."

Jack didn't say anything for the rest of the lunch period, just munched his biscuit bread and peanut butter and looked mean. Everyone knew he would probably never go north to his post-office job.

Jack Bowen didn't seem like most brothers to Dandy. He didn't make threats or get angry when Marie Ann first showed interest in him. Lots of times Jack would daydream aloud with Dandy. He would tell how he would one day visit Dandy in the city, and maybe not go back to Mary's Shore. Secretly, Dandy knew Jack dreamed of

visiting him and Marie Ann in their home in the wonderful city. But, nevertheless, they were real friends;
they had mutual enemies.

"That goddamned Uncle Clyde is goin' ta git it one
day," Jack said.

"What happened?"

"Wahl he just rides me, that's all. I was on the second floor of the mill today stackin' boxes like Mr. Harvey Wentley told me and Uncle Clyde came on up there
and pulled me off the job."

"Yeah? That sounds bad."

"Sho nuf, hope ma gonna die but Harvey like ta
pitched a bitch when he saw me traipsin' my pretty
black self down there on the mill floor amongst all them
white gals."

"Yeah, I hear he don't like none of the young fellows
ta be down dere near the girls, not even with himself
dere."

"That sho is right; Uncle Clyde is harmless; that's
why he's foreman, but if he don't always stop fukkin' wit
me . . . I'm goin' ta knock his ole rusty ass off."

They neared the rear of the outhouse and fell silent
because they didn't know who might be inside.

After they passed, Jack said: "Junior Kane is comin' over, gonna go ov'va ta his place for some boozin'
tonight."

"Yeah?"

"How 'bout goin'?"

"Why sho nuf, Mr. Bowen."

Junior Kane had a '34 Chevy and three half-sisters.
The girls were young enough for Dandy and all attrac-
tive in their big-eyed, slow-talkin' country ways. Their

reputations were of being fast girls for that part of the world.

Jack pulled out a pack of Chesterfields. He offered Dandy one and they lit up. Dandy didn't like to smoke. Before he began training, he smoked just enough to let his gang know that he did and after, he almost stopped completely. Since he had come down to Mt. Holy on his second vacation, he smoked whenever offered.

They walked into the kitchen, cigarettes in mouths. Uncle Clyde and Aunt Bessie were fussing.

"Now when I tell these little boys ta do somethin', Bessie, I meant it, ya hear?"

"These kids ain't for you to be always jumpin' on whenever you get ready, Clyde."

Marie Ann stood beside the sink with a dish towel and gave approving looks to Aunt Bessie. Ida was over the sink with elbows in suds, softly singing a gospel song.

Jack and Dandy crept through the kitchen, crossed the front room and climbed the second floor to their room. They passed Marie Ann and Ida's room first, then a spare room that was used when more guests arrived or during camp-meeting times when the house was jammed, and reached their large room at the end of the hall which ran the length of the house and had four large beds and a double-decker that Roy and Richard preferred to sleep in.

Jack stretched out on his bed and Dandy sat on his, reaching for a Western magazine on the nightstand between them.

"The Durango Kid sure gits into it, don't he?" Dandy commented.

Jack peered over his arms and said: "Sho do, I couldn't

put that book there down until I had found out how the showdown would come off."

A tramping upon the stairs was heard.

"Stop it, Fatso," a cry came before the speeding tumble of tennis shoes.

"Hee heee heee . . ."

Roy and Richard burst around the corner at the stair's top, and Richard chased the giggling boy down the hallway, into the bedroom.

Roy pulled himself into a corner between wall, bureau and bed, and Richard, like a small scarecrow, thrashed at him with half-hearted pokes of his fists.

"Heee heee . . . Oooo, man," Roy called to his antagonist, "Fatso, stop!"

"Yeah, stop it, goddammit," Jack shouted.

"Oh, Bo," his brother protested. "Bo, he's always botherin' me."

"Heee . . . dat ain't right, Bowen," Roy said.

"SHUT UP, BOTH OF YOU! I DON'T WANT TA HEAR ANY MORE OF IT!"

Richard stepped away from the hole where Roy crouched and grumbled as he searched through a drawer. Roy came out, hand over mouth, strangling on his laughs, and finally hid his head under the double-decked bed, pretending to look for shoes.

"You guys goin' to choir meetin'?" Dandy asked the younger boys.

"Yeah, Dandy," Richard said. "We goin' but I don't know if'in we'll stay in the choir."

"Fatso's startin' a quartet," Roy spoke out.

"A quartet?" Jack said. "What makes ya think ya can sing?"

"Well, it's like dis, Bo," one of them began. And they took the next half hour while changing their clothes to describe the gospel quartet they were starting and how when they were good enough their group, The Mt. Holy Four, would go on nationwide tours, even to New York City and Philly.

"Why don't you come on out and try to get on at the mill tomorrow, Dandy?" Jack said after the boys had gone downstairs.

"Oh, I'd like ta, Jack, but you remember the kiddin' I got when I quit the chicken plant after three days."

"Awww, forgit that," Jack said. "Remember I quit two days later."

"Yeah, but you work all the time and I don't even have ta unless I want ta have extra money."

"I know, but you're gittin' pretty tired 'round here all day listenin' to Bessie . . . Say, are ya makin' much time with mah little sister?" There was a guarded flash in his eyes.

"Nawh, not much," Dandy said. "Aunt Bessie is around all da time."

"Well, ya shouldn't mind comin' down ta da plant then. Thar's ah couple ah nice gals down there, and you can always take Marie Ann ta the movies in Dover on Saturday nights."

"I'll ask Aunt Bessie."

A car chugged into the driveway; its wheezing engine clanged in time to the barks and yips and prancing of the newly unleashed dogs. The car's horn went *ahhh hunnggaaa ahhh hunnggaaa ahhh hunnggaaa* before the brittle pinging of the girls' giggles rose above Aunt Bessie's voice bellowing welcomes to Junior Kane from the kitchen window.

Downstairs, Dandy stopped in the kitchen with Aunt Bess and Uncle Clyde as Jack strolled out to the car surrounded by the girls and two small boys on the old running boards.

"Howdy dere, Bowen," the driver yelled.

"Wahll if'n it ain't dat mule thief, Bro Kane."

The girls laughed more; their soft and syrupy drawls oozed over the heavy evening air as the sky glowed pink and violet and above trees to the east, twilight was promised by the gleam of a full moon on a pale blue-purple horizon.

"I'm goin' down ta the mill with Jack tomorrow, Aunt Bessie," Dandy said.

"Okay, son," the old woman answered.

"Wha' ya say, Dandy?" the old man asked.

"I'm goin ta try an' get on at da mill, Uncle Clyde."

"Shssucks . . . who you tryin' ta fool, boy? You don't wan'ta work."

"Ain't none of your business, Clyde," Aunt Bess said.

"Oh, dammit, Bessie! I don't care what he does but he better know he's gon'na work when he's on mah crew. I don't play no favorites."

"We know you don't play favorites, Clyde," the woman said. "You'd work your mama to death if that white man wanted ya."

"NOW LISSEN HERE, BESSIE!"

Dandy went out the door and over to the car. Jack sat in the front next to the driver and the remainder of the group stood by the windows.

"Howdy dere, Dandy," the driver said.

"Hi, Junior."

"What's goin' on with you, Dandy?"

"Wahll, I guess I'll be workin' with you guys startin' tomorrow."

Excitement rose with everyone having something to add about Dandy's decision. Finally, Marie Ann went into the house, soon followed by Ida.

"Ain't you boys goin' ta choir rehearsal?" Dandy asked.

"Yeah, we goin' as soon as Ida gits ready. Shucks, she's been out hare makin' eyes at Junior Kane hare an' makin' us late."

Junior was a sun-darkened wiry boy in his late teens. He spoke with a coarse accent and laughed a lot.

"Stop dat fibbin'," Jack said. "You knows Marie Ann has got Junior all staked out." Dandy saw Jack wink at him from behind Junior Kane's head. Junior broke into a great grin and showed tobacco-stained teeth.

"But Bo!" one of the little boys protested.

"Shut up! Don't let me hear anything 'bout nobody flirtin' wit' Marie Ann's boyfriend."

"Here she comes."

Ida came out of the house wearing a red full-length coat. The hue heightened her bright skin and caused her teeth to flash within the scarlet-smeared mouth. She waved at Aunt Bessie through the kitchen-door window and turned toward the car and her admirers.

"See you, Junior," she said and waved. "See you when I git home, Dandy and Bo." She hurried down the drive. "Come on, you little boys," she called while the two pups wagged their ends behind her heels.

"I'll race ya to Ida, Fatso."

"Oooo, man, we better catch her before she gets by the cemetery, or Aunt Bess will get on us."

And the boys were gone down the drive, laughing and squealing to the mingled barking of the dogs and the threatening yells of Ida.

Dandy opened the rear door and crawled in the back.

"Want a cigarette, Dandy?" Junior offered.

"Wow, a Raleigh!"

"Yeah, I save the coupons."

The radio played country music.

Rocks are mah cradle . . . da cole ground's mah bed . . . da highway's mah home and I's might as well be dead . . .

Night came soon and the lights shone from the kitchen window and upstairs in Marie Ann's room. From under the seat Junior pulled four quarts of beer and opened each with a minimum of fizzing and handed Jack and Dandy one bottle.

"Ohhheee, Kane, you're really goin' ta do it tonight, boy," Jack said.

"Them sisters of mine have got some home brew ready and we might as well git primed."

Thar I go . . . thar I go . . . thaaare I goo'oh . . . purty baby you's's de soul that snaps mah control . . .

Marie Ann came out of the house wearing fresh short shorts and a white blouse outlining her young breasts.

"Ya ready ta go, Marie?" Junior asked as she got in the back of the car next to Dandy.

"Nawh, I didn't go ta choir meetin' and I better not go with yawhl."

"Why not, Marie? Jack will be dere." Junior handed her the last quart of beer and she peered into the kitchen window to see if the old folks sat at the table. Aunt Bess and Uncle Clyde were in the front of the house; they sat in their bedroom off of the living room or watched television. Marie sipped at the beer. "Damn, this is good." She leaned her elbows across the top of the front seat and placed her head between the half-turned heads of her brother and her boyfriend, Junior Kane.

"Sho gits dark quick around here," she said.

And night was outside, enclosing the blackened car as the pitter patter of the returning dogs' feet came from the road, and the cricket music and an occasional pig's oink and a drowsy duck quacked at the dark, while the white summer moon swung up into the black, star-pierced southern heavens, and the stars that no city lights dimmed, winked as if they too had secrets.

Wha ain't ya out'in da forest fighten' dose grea' big ole grizzly bears?

I's a lady!

Dey got lady bears out dere.

"Dandy, you'll like it down the mill," Jack said.

"Ya sho will, boy," Junior Kane said. "Mr. Harvey Wentley's sho nice ta git along wit'."

"I'm sho glad you goin', Dandy," Marie Ann teased. "Get real tired ah seein' yo face 'round here all the time."

Dandy's hand moved across the seat and caressed her bare legs; she flinched but took another sip of beer. Dandy had his bottle between his knees and drew on one of the cigarettes he took from Junior.

"Ya gonna buy me one of them great big straw hats when ya git paid, Dandy?" Marie asked.

"One ah them Texas ones . . . shore will, Marie. I don't want ya ta git any blacker," he teased. "I'll git one with a string on it so ya can drop it back over ya neck and let ya hair fly."

"Ya never asked me fo ah ten-gallon straw hat, Marie Ann," Junior said.

And the music played.

I found mah thrill on Blueberry Hill . . . on Blueberry Hill . . . where I found you . . .

"How's Ethel gittin' along?" Jack asked Junior.

"Oeewee, she's fit to be tied. Daisy and Helen came down ta da mill, ya know, and got on. Now dere camp-meetin' outfits' gonna be as purty as hers."

"Sho nuff?" Jack said.

"Hee heee . . ." Marie Ann simpered.

"Ah most like ta died too when I heard, Marie," Junior said.

"Ahm jest glad I don' have ta work . . . got mah ole big bro here," she said and caressed her brother's arm.

Dandy's fingers in the dark had crawled under the band of her shorts and squeezed between the firm thighs and around between the soft lips of the swelling labium. She squirmed and hunched nearer her boyfriend and rested her head upon her brother's shoulder.

"What y'all keep gigglin' fo, Marie Ann?" Junior Kane asked.

"This is really some good beer," she said as she willed herself to restrain the shudder which reached from her center, and she opened her legs wide in the near-total blackness and rested the rear end of her tight bottom on the cushion and leaned fully forward with her knees bent and her arms supporting herself.

"Give me a cigarette, Junior, pleez," she asked.

"I didn't know you did all this, gal," Junior kidded and giggled with her as he fished for his pack.

Marie Ann stretched farther over so that the light of the match would not reach over the rim of the car seat, and Dandy's moist moving finger flickered over her pursy clitoris.

"Ummm . . ." she said and hunched even farther forward.

"Wha you say, Marie?" Junior Kane asked.

"Just thinkin' . . ." she said.

Dandy took another long swallow of his beer, nearly finishing the bottle. Jack tilted his up and Junior got bold enough to twist about and kiss Marie Ann full in the mouth.

"Ummm . . ." she said between her lips and Dandy's finger worked like a lever. "Ohhh . . . that's so good," she said as Junior pressed harder. Dandy wondered how the two in front could not detect the heavy sweet funk odor.

"Whatcha doin' ta mah baby sister?" Jack Bowen kidded in the dark. "Dandy, boy, you sittin' back dere and lettin' Junior git away with the goods."

"Yeah, Junior's really makin' out," Dandy said.

"Shusss . . . ooeee . . . ummm . . ." Marie said and wriggled too much and lifted her girlish rear fully off the backseat.

"Owww . . . Marie Ann," Junior Kane cried. "You

know how ta French kiss. Where did ya larn ta use yo tongue like dat?"

"Okay, children," Jack spoke up and put his hand on Junior's shoulder. "That's enough for tonight."

Marie Ann sat back and gave a convulsive tremble as she lowered herself fully upon Dandy's hand.

"Wha'cha shiverin' fo, Marie?" Junior asked as she grabbed his hands and arm. "Bowen," he called out, "dis y'ere lil beer's got dis gal high as a Georgia pine."

And the radio never stopped.

Mah pappa's a jockey an he teach me how ta ride . . .
Oh, yeah, mah pappa's a jockey an he teach me how ta
ride . . . He said git in'da middle son an' ya move from
side to side . . .

"I have ta go," Marie said. She jerked across the seat and stepped out. "Good night, Dandy."

"Good night, Marie Ann," Junior called.

"Night, Junior."

The screen door slapped shut and the boys in the car were quiet. A pig squealed from the pens and the darkness chirped with crickets.

I's wan' ah bowlegg'd w'man dat's all . . . I's wan ah
bowlegg'd woman dat's tall . . .

"Sho was a good starter fo tonight," Junior said and lifted the last of his beer. "Here's the rest of Marie's, Dandy, why don't ya finish it."

"Thanks, partner."

"Whall, let's be gittin' whare we ain't," Jack urged.

"Okay thar," Junior yelled and turned on the ignition.

"Whall, that leaves me out, fellows," Dandy said and stepped into the yard. The dogs trotted up to him and wagged their tails in the moonlight, their eyes glistening yellow in the dark.

"Wha'cha say, Dandy?" Junior asked. "I thought ya was comin' wit' us."

"Can't. Startin' at the mill tomorrow and the first day is always hell. It's almost eight now and I'll have ta get up at five-thirty."

"Shit," Jack said. "So do we."

"Yeah, but you're ust'ta it."

"Awww, c'mon, Dandy. I promised Helen I would bring ya back. She's fixin' up all fo ya," Junior said.

"Nawh . . . can't do it. I'll see her tomorrow at work and explain."

. . . wit' her big bowlegs so wide apart . . .

The tail lights of the '34 Chevy dipped up the road as the old car banged over potholes. Dandy entered the house and looked back through the screen at the two red lights jerking away.

"Good night, Uncle Clyde," Dandy said as he passed the old man sitting before the television screen, the set almost booming.

"I thought you were goin' with Jack and Junior," the old man said. "Your Aunt Bessie went ta sleep because she thought everybody was out."

"Nawh, have ta start work in the morning, so I better get some sleep."

"Whal, son . . . I didn't know ya had dat much sense."

The old woman slept, Dandy thought, because she didn't know anyone would be home but her and the old man. If she had known that Marie and he would be alone . . .

Dandy passed the girls' room; doorless, the entrance framed Marie lying face down upon the bed with her head toward the window.

Dandy went to his room and untied his shoes and let them drop loudly upon the floor. Then he undressed and changed into his pajamas. Later, with lights out, he tiptoed down the hallway and into the girls' room.

"*Dandy, no!*" Marie whispered when he turned her over on her back.

He put his finger to his lips and then tipped back to the door and clicked off the light. Moonlight spilled over the girl, her white blouse catching the light and showing dark valleys below her breasts.

"*No, Dandy,*" she whispered, "*Aunt Bess will hear.*"

"*She's asleep!*"

"*Uncle Clyde!*"

"*You know he can't hear so good.*"

"No, Dandy, I can't," she murmured as he unbuttoned her shorts and pulled them with her panties down over her knees, down her brown moon-revealed thighs, down her long night-exposed legs to her tennis shoes.

She clamped her feet tight. Dandy tried to pry them apart, but she held them with all her strength and he couldn't get them apart unless he forced her with all his power.

The moonlight moved down over her brown body. Dandy moved up and kissed her lips as she rolled her head from side to side, and he kissed her shut eyes as she rolled her head, the muscles taut in her neck, and finally, after the pure white blouse was gone and the brassiere, he suckled her breasts in his starved mouth as her head shook no no no no no.

"*No, Dandy, you gonna com' in me!*"

"*No, darling, I'll use protection,*" he said. "*Don't you understand I love you? I'll take care of you. Trust me!*"

"*I'm sorry, Dandy. I can't. I just can't. I'm so sorry!*"

Half an hour later, twin tear streaks running from Marie's eyes caught the moonlight and dripped into her matted hair and dampened the pillows and spread, and Dandy felt like adding to the deluge, for he had gotten no further in his conquest than inserting the same practiced finger and making the girl's dark nipples stand out like buttons. His finger worked and his lips worked kissing away the tears and warming the tight eyelids and peppering the little nipple with pecks. His lips also pleaded in low prayer to the beautiful brown animal, and his eyes helped by the full moon fixed for moments on the curling pubic hair above his hand.

"*Ahm sorry, Dandy; don't be mad at me . . . Will ya still git me the Texas hat?*"

And the video still blared below.

Tonight we bring you the passionate saga of love and . . .

When Richard and Roy and Ida climbed the stairs to their bedrooms, Dandy had rolled Marie under the covers but had done little else.

"Good night," Aunt Bessie called up. "Is everybody home now?"

"Yes ma'am," Ida replied. "All cept'n Bo and Dandy."

"I'm goin' ta be da greatest lead tenor on da Eastern Shore," Roy promised.

"Awww, man, you ain't gonna be nothin'," Richard said as they passed the girls' doorway. "A chicken can crow better den you."

"Shut up, you little boys," Ida warned and stepped into her room. "Don't be makin' a lot of fuss."

"*Don't turn that light on, Ida,*" Marie Ann said.

The moon had been lost somewhere above the Mt. Holy church steeple when Jack Bowen crept up the stairs, slipped past his sister's and Ida's room and sat on his bed.

"Damn . . ." he said. "Where's Dandy?"

"Heee . . . heee . . ."

"Wha ya say, Roy?" he asked.

"Yeah, Bo . . . heee heee . . ."

"Oooo, man, shut up," Richard warned.

"Well, I'll be damned," Jack said softly and slipped under the covers.

Down the hall, the bed in the girls' room squeaked barely when a violent movement was made.

"*Ohhh . . . ohhh . . . Dandy,*" Ida James whimpered. "*I love you.*"

"Shusss . . ." he shushed her.

Marie Ann whimpered in her sleep, a captive in a bad dream, and beside her Dandy clutched the big yaller hot-as-a-ten-cent-pistol-gal to himself and worried about how he would tell Jack Bowen in the morning that he had never touched his baby sister.